Franc... professional life
pract... ...ich has informed
her h... ...e has been the
recipi... ...ver Crime Writers'
Asso... ...regular broadcaster on
Radio... ...er of the series 'Tales
from... ...n and in Deal, over-
looki... ...ion

Also by Frances Fyfield

Helen West series

A Question of Guilt

Trial by Fire

Deep Sleep

Shadow Play

A Clear Conscience

Without Consent

Sarah Fortune series

Shadows on the Mirror

Perfectly Pure and Good

Staring at the Light

Looking Down

Safer Than Houses

Diana Porteous series

Gold Digger

Casting the First Stone

A Painted Smile

Other fiction

The Playroom

Half Light

Let's Dance

Blind Date

Undercurrents

The Nature of the Beast

Seeking Sanctuary

The Art of Drowning

Blood From Stone

Cold to the Touch

CASTING THE FIRST STONE

FRANCES FYFIELD

SPHERE

First published in Great Britain in 2013 by Sphere
This paperback edition published in 2014 by Sphere

3 5 7 9 10 8 6 4 2

Copyright © Frances Fyfield 2013

The moral right of the author has been asserted.

A CIP catalogue record for this book
is available from the British Library.

ISBN 978-0-7515-4969-0

Typeset in Plantin by MRules
Printed and bound in Great Britain by
Clays Ltd, St Ives plc

Papers used by Sphere are from well-managed forests
and other responsible sources.

Sphere
An imprint of
Little, Brown Book Group
Carmelite House
50 Victoria Embankment
London EC4Y 0DZ

An Hachette UK Company
www.hachette.co.uk

www.littlebrown.co.uk

For Audrey Roethenbaugh,
Artist and reader

PROLOGUE

There they were, like a herd of elephants. Three diggers on the beach.

Like mechanical monsters, capable of anything.

The first machine was bigger than a desert tank. Amphibious, oh yes, it has tracks that could flatten a road. It could crush your head and grind it into dust; it could flatten a body into a pancake, like something out of a cartoon. Popeye, squashed. The task of the yellow machines was to move a million tons of shingle. Some were flint, way harder than bone, shaped to resist. Rounded stones, rough stones, slid from beneath the giant tracks of the elephant; they moved, they evaded, too strong, too worn to crack. The amphibious monster could swivel on itself, bend its huge neck and pick up two tons at a time, swing it round and drop it somewhere else within the parameters of its long beak. Pterodactyl, monolithic elephant, almost friendly and if alive, maybe a vegetarian with a diet of whole trees and mountains. The shovel at the end of its long swivel head could nod, say hello, consider the problem, look worried, and then bury itself deep into the shingle, like something hunting prey. Up it came with a colossal jaw full of stone, lingered for a moment, turned round and redistributed the whole parcel with enormous grace. Not my problem, not this load, not any more, it seemed to say. Children and adults stood transfixed behind the railings, watching. Dogs barked, disturbed, but for the rest, there was nothing better than a big, swaggering machine.

They were transferring shingle from the dredger, far out, up a pipe and on to shore. The pipe itself was twelve feet in diameter, spouting forth stones of different colours in a flood of brown water. Occasionally, the machinery went into remission, spouting forth pure water to cleanse itself. It all looked God-like, as if the beach were being recreated instead of a mere, futile fight against nature. The shingle had withdrawn downwards into the bed of the sea, year in, year out. The withdrawal undermined the sea wall, so they said, and every few years, *they* defy the process, replace the stone with more stone for the sea to reclaim all over again. These clumsy, powerful elephants with their sensitive trunks, working in a jungle of stone and water. Such lordly creatures.

Spectators found favourites, based on observation. There was the biggest digger with the most sensitive nose and the best operator, the one who swallowed the maximum amount into the shovel and dropped the least. That one waited a second more before he released the load, getting his great big mouth to drop it slowly without dribbling, before the jaw swung back, utterly empty. The other one was just a little clumsier. Only a small difference. The big one (and people on shore stared lasciviously at the driver of this beast – he did not respond, although aware of the audience), was the one that moved the pipe that pumped the shingle ashore. He did it delicately. The mouth lowered a chain onto the pipe. The jaw of the beast picked up the chain in its teeth, threw it to one side, then picked it up again, lifted it over the pipe gently and, almost accidentally, locked it. Then moved the pipe gently, sideways.

Then, Digger Two came in, the clumsier one, shuffled the pipe with its nose, bolstered it up with a few tons of shingle so that the whole direction of the thing turned east, and laid itself on the ballast of a new slope. The big guy did the delicate business of shuffling the pipes into alignment, so that the whole force of the flow of water and shingle altered to another place, while in the meantime, Digger Three, a different beast with no jaws, no high-elevation mouth, shovelled away. That one was the earth-shovelling badger, with a broad front and a tank engine powering up the back. It ploughed into stuff, ploughed through waves, ploughed through the fountain of shingle coming out of that pipe and pushed it around. It hit the flow, knew its depth, pushed away tons in the flat shovel at the front, running through water. Together, they created a bank of what had been pumped up out of the sea. Then they nuzzled about, the badger digger and the two, snouted, removers, smoothing the mixture of stone and sand into manageable shapes. They nudged it with their soft noses and their variable skills: the diggers snorted, retreated, advanced, ploughed. They disregarded the wind and the weather. It was nothing to them.

Once the tide had fallen, and they had paused, they would talk to the people watching at the railings. Mostly, they came from Rotterdam, speaking gentle, der de der English. And der next week, we level the beach, ya, only in two days, we go home to Rotterdam for a new crew. Three days off.

4

And the machines? They stay here? Of course. Our elephants, ya? They will be guarded, ya. I shouldn't trust yourself ashore, mate, one man says. Go to the pub and the women will be all over you, to say nothing of the men. Har har. No, we mostly stay on the ship. Good boys, good food. Big bonus if we do it to time. Big, big, bonus. Only someone stays on the shore to guard the elephants and get us going in the morning.

The operator man who was not quite as good as the other one, the one with the slightly smaller crane, who sometimes slithered around and dribbled the load, was the only one of the crane men who stayed ashore. That one. He said he wanted to stay with the night watchman who slept in the hut alongside the compound where the machines rested overnight at the far end of the beach, guarded by a high, spotlit fence. Just to help, he said. Stretch my legs, too. There was a lust for these machines: they were priceless and people came to worship them. Stefan thought they could look after themselves and, having locked eyes with someone who watched him so admiringly from beyond the barriers, he had another agenda, secured by a smile and a gesture.

The noise was not so bad, even at night. Digging, not drilling, more of a subdued roaring, a distant, vibrant, irregular grumbling. The pipe could only pump on to the beach at high tide; once the tide turned, pumping stopped, leaving mountains of wet shingle like a new range of hills. It was the silence that startled and at dawn, a new view. Mountains of shingle to be levelled out tomorrow and the day after that, night and day, covering the old with the new.

Not so very far away, but in another world, a rich young man called Steven failed to sleep and thought of the sea and the place where he was born. Where he wanted to return, but couldn't yet, not until he knew who his mother was. All he knew about his birth was that his father had presented his infertile wife with his own, locally got bastard when she came down to the village to join him in the place where he had decided they should live. And the wife had taken him, legitimised him, and loved him too much.

What he did not know was if he had been stolen, or given, or rejected. It should not matter now, but it did. It loomed large; it meant that while he had everything, he had nothing, because he did not know who he was.

He looked at the painting in his hands and let it bring the sea closer. Wondering if the sea would look and feel the same when he saw it next.

Janek would be round soon.

PART ONE

CHAPTER ONE

Picture. *A hot day on a steep shingle beach.*

What is going on here, said the green Frog?
I don't know, said the Witch.
I don't know Which from Witch, said the Frog
And lay down sideways while
The witch tickled his tummy
Before they slid into the Pond
And thought about other things.
He thought about fish and
She thought about bones.
Do fish eat bones?

'I'm sure they do,' Patrick said. 'They eat anything, don't they?'

'I'm not sure,' Di said, alarmed that she might have given something away in this half-asleep game they were playing. Just say whatever comes into your head. 'Did I mention bones?'

'Yes. We were doing one line each. We were trying to make a poem.'

'So we were,' she said.

'To encourage the fish, you said. Something like that, only it's not working, is it? And I'm hungry.'

Di rubbed sleep from her eyes.

They were sitting on the shingle beach below the big house. The beach was steep, reconfigured after the winter storms, and the house itself was out of sight from where they sprawled next to their fishing rods on the warm stones. All memory of biting, skin-stripping wind was forgotten: it was as if it was always like this and always would be; calm, clear, hot, with the water mimicking a breathing pond and speaking nicely instead of shouting at them. The worst possible conditions for catching fish, but then the fishing rods were only an excuse for a rich widow and her late husband's twelve-year-old grandson to lie around getting brown and playing silly word games while half asleep.

Patrick's mother would not approve but Patrick's mother was not there to shield her child from the sun. Still, it was time he went indoors.

Life was such a contrast at this end of the beach furthest from the town, left unscathed by the recent flood-defence work on the shore north of the pier. Those huge machines had moved on, although as long as they had been there, Patrick had defected from home and raced to watch, transfixed by them. He had drawn them, examined them, cross-examined them, spoken to their ears and remained mesmerised. Di feared that his ambition to be an artist had become subsumed into a fervent desire to become the driver of the biggest earth-shifting machinery in the world, training to begin as soon as possible. Let it be: it was a noble ambition and he had also succumbed to the peace of this day, throwing stones and dreaming of fishes. The spectacle of the diggers and the cranes was something Di had enjoyed, too. Peg, de facto housekeeper at Di's mansion, and relatively newly released from a short prison sentence, had enjoyed it even more. Immoderately, Saul would have said, but only as much as half the town who had come out in fine weather to be entertained for three weeks. Some said it was a shameful waste; the sea would reclaim it all. Di liked the idea of Patrick being an engineer or driver better than she liked the idea of him becoming an artist. Vocations were all inevitable routes towards breaking your heart – better have some fun. She shook herself. Depression seemed endemic. Grief made her sour.

She sat up and brushed thick hair from her eyes. Her hair was bleached gold with streaks of other colours in it, a bit ratty for a respectable young widow whose hair should not be so neglected. Old cut-off jeans and a raggy T-shirt was uniform for the beach. She loved getting dirty in clothes unsuitable for the other parts of life which, today at least, were postponed. The salerooms and the shops of a distant city did not beckon and the discomfort of the stony beach was paradise.

Bones, though; what to do about the bones?

Still rubbing her eyes in a daze of irresponsibility and turning back towards the house, looking at the brow of the beach in the hazy heat, she saw him. He was sitting in his dark clothing, maybe fifty yards down, looking out to sea and quietly drawing attention to himself by simply waiting. Di felt the familiar stab of raw fear, followed by something more akin to weary resignation; an absence of fear: the realisation that she was safe from him. Less fear than loathing, at any rate. Maybe that was depression, too. He had nothing to gain from harming her and he would not take the risk. Her father never did anything head on, never attacked in an open space, or at all. He sidled round the edges, and besides, she could run far faster than him.

Patrick yawned. Late afternoon, going home tomorrow. Food needed, as always. There was the litter of the last snacks scattered around him.

'You go back up to the house and find Peg,' Di said. 'You can peel the potatoes, the pair of you. Take out the rubbish.'

'Be useful,' he said. 'No food gets on the table without someone cooking it, right? OK?' He yawned and stretched. 'Are you staying a bit longer?'

'Yes, just a bit.'

As soon as Patrick had taken his lanky long legs over the bank and out of sight, the man in the dark clothes got up and moved towards Di. It took a little effort for her father to limp over the shingle; she could hear him long before he was close. Slush, crunch, swearing under his breath when he slipped. She found his difficulty as satisfying as it was reassuring and she hoped it was painful. There was no way he could sneak up on her and stick a knife in her back. Not his style, anyway; her father, known as Quig, could only skin an animal if someone had slaughtered it for him. He sat down heavily and groaned and he might, just might, be putting it on. Hardly an old man yet, not out of his fifties, not nearly as old as her husband Thomas had been. Thomas had been almost seventy when he died the year before, and yet in comparison to this bent, pale creature, he had been as sleek and dark as an otter and, to her eyes, as handsome as ever was. Diana Porteous, nee Quigly, wondered if there had ever been a time when she had revered her father half as much.

'Hello, daughter mine,' the man said. 'Isn't it time we talked?'

She had not really heard his voice in years. There had been a sentence in her ear, that night last year, when he had stolen into the house, and that might have been mere imagination. His voice was surprisingly clear. She said nothing, listening intently to the muttering of the sea and looking at her hands, no longer able to hate him with the old intensity. Hatred? What was that? Something she found impossible to sustain; even for her husband's children, who had come near to murdering her on that same night when dear old Dad came in. Contempt was another matter and yet she had scant supply of that, too. She had no moral right to it. Two years in prison had quite squeezed it out of her, long before she had nursed a dying husband whom nobody believed she had loved to extinction.

'I don't see why we should talk. What do we have to talk about? You buggered off when I was fourteen. You sold me to a thief. I've scarcely seen you since. Only in the distance.'

He shuffled closer, not too close. She tensed herself to rise and run, settled back and touched the warm stones.

'Ah yes, but you were a good little thief already. And didn't I do you a favour? Look how well it turned out for you.'

She said nothing.

'You really couldn't have done better,' he continued. 'First you burgle a rich man's house. Old and rich. You made a great impression on the old pervert, so good that he invites you back. Then he marries you, and leaves you all this. Oh yes, I did you a favour. I gave you a great head start.'

The taunt in his voice; she remembered it well. Remembered, that however inarticulate he was, he still had a way with words as lethal as his fist, his knife, his gun. He was her surviving parent, so different from her gentle mother, but still with a hypodermic needle in one of her veins. She fingered one of the larger stones and gripped it. So easy to spring up and crash a stone into his head, use it to cripple an ankle; it was him who had taught her the

15

possibility. Bloodless or bloody: either way, she could wash off the stains in the sea. The voice of him undermined her.

'Didn't the girl do well?' he went on. 'Look at you. Richest bitch in the neighbourhood. Owner of a collection of fine art and a fine house with at least fifteen bedrooms, sea view and everything. Mistress of all she surveys. Well, nothing dries soonest than a woman's tears. A good little thief, who burgles a poor old man, steals his heart, comes back and steals the rest. Gets all this.'

Di fingered the large round stone once more, dropped it gently. Then she picked up another one and held it in both hands. Looking down towards the shore, she could see the ghost of Thomas, climbing out of the water and waving, that long, lean, elderly body which had been a source of wonder to her. Thomas seemed to have mastery of the sea. All their passions were shared.

Don't do it, Di. You can't go back to prison. You are not going to go back to that place for someone who is cunning, but stupid. If her father had been a truly clever man, he would never have insulted her husband, never have sneered. He would have flattered her. She dropped the stone. Little point explaining to him what it had been like, or that yes, she had been sent to the house of Thomas Porteous to steal from him, and yes, she had subsequently married him. They had married one another and only death would have parted them. No point explaining because he already knew; might even know how much she had loved him. No, he would never know that.

'What do you want?' she said.

'I only want to help,' he said. 'You can't move on until you deal with them bones.'

'Which bones are they?' she said, articulating clearly, the way Thomas had and she now did.

'The bones,' he said. 'The bones in the cellar. I know they're there. No one else can help you but me. *Her* bones.'

Diana the huntress picked up the largest stone she could find, rose to her feet in a fluid movement and flung it overarm into the sea. That way, she could illustrate how strong she was and how much she could have hurt him if she tried.

'I can help you with them bones.'

'Which bones?' she repeated.

'Her bones. The ones you dream about.'

'I don't dream of bones, Father. I dream of other things.'

Di left him there, took her own long legs up the shingle bank and did not look back to see him struggling.

And yet the urge to throw the stone and make it

17

connect with his head was an urge that remained, because so much of what he said was true. He knew where she came from; she had his genes, too.

Back at the house, Patrick said to Peg, 'What's wrong with her? What's wrong with my auntie, the wicked witch?'

Peg was mightily pleased with herself today, had been all week.

'Isn't nothing wrong with her, she's a star, you know that. If you don't know that, you don't know nothing. And she isn't your auntie, she's your granddad's second wife. Work it out.'

'Whatever. She's great.'

'Right, young man, that's all you need to know. Get peeling potatoes, willya? You know chips are better done from raw. And we gotta do something different for Saul, cos he's here this evening. Already got in and gone upstairs. Don't like chips, the silly ponce.

'What was wrong with her on the beach, anyway?'

'She kept drifting off.'

'So? Didn't you?'

'Yes.'

'There you go then. It's the heat. We aren't used to it.'

'And then there was this man, watching us. I know him,

I've seen him before, I drew a picture of him. I left her down there with him. I shouldn't have . . . '

'Man with a limp and a hat?'

Patrick nodded.

'No worries about *him*, sunshine. No worries at all. What about my worries, hey? My only worries is how soon you're gonna come back my great big tall man. Soon, hey?'

Patrick drove himself into her, colliding in a massive embrace which had his head enveloped in her big bosom, so that it was cushioned while his arms were wrapped round her waist and his feet left the ground. They growled at one another in a code of noises and swung each other round like a pair of fighters about to land on a mat. Then, having got the best of each other, they had a friendly snarl and detached, laughing and hitting.

'Get outta here,' she said. 'Get in the shower. You stink of seaweed.'

'You stink of fish,' he said.

'Get washed, boy.'

Laughter, that was what they had over supper on a balmy night. The most unlikely people, some might say. There was Di, looking like sand, as if she had grown out of it; there was Saul, tall, effete, skinny and dressed for dinner in a linen ensemble, sniffing his salts and sipping his wine;

there was Peg, all blousy and frilly and curvy; and last in, Jones, Di's sort of uncle, watchdog, whatever, drinking beer, talking about the fish he had caught, and they were eating home-made chips and salad with herbs from the back yard and Patrick holding forth, chattering like the sparrows he had heard at dawn.

This was home, the only one they knew.

Patrick did not know about the bones in the cellar. He was the only one who did not know, although the others assumed that Peg remained in ignorance. All of them, apart from Saul, were a little hazy about the potential value of the paintings hanging on the walls. Who knew how much? None of them quite knew what they wanted to do next, apart from Patrick, who was certain about the short term: buy a crane and drive it. Otherwise, he wanted to sketch the birds in the bay before he went home tomorrow; wanted to catch them in flight. And next time, go out in a boat.

Di wondered where her father would sleep that night. Perhaps he was under the pier.

Bones and stones were the subject of her dreams.

CHAPTER TWO

Dammit, write it down.

The only cure for disturbing dreams and lethargy was writing it down. The morning after Patrick left, Di found herself tapping out the story on the keys, as if she was explaining it to him. She preferred to write when everyone else was asleep.

This is how it was, Di wrote on her computer, that bible of her memories, remember to write succinctly. People are easily bored. Write something every day.

She had to type it out, as if explaining it to a stranger. One day Patrick would read this. It was a history she often revised, so as to understand it herself.

I was an undersized sixteen-year-old when I came to burgle

*Thomas Porteous on the night of the storm, eleven years ago.
I was sent in to steal the keys to his car, and anything else small
and precious I could find. I couldn't do it. I saw Thomas tied
to his chair. Christina, his ex wife, had come to call, pleading
for money which was refused. She was mad with envy; she
planned to burn his house down, with him in it. The fire was
prepared in the cellar. I heard her run away when I came in,
and that was all I heard over the storm, apart from Thomas's
voice, telling me to go.*

*I didn't go: I cut the bonds on his wrists, and then the police
came, and I said nothing.*

Di sat back, depression winning. Talked it through to
herself.

Thomas's wife went down to the cellar to hide. It had
filled with sudden water, and she drowned. While I was in
prison, Thomas blocked off her end of the cellar, and left
her there. He never wanted her daughters to know how
mad and bad she was. In order to get custody of her children when she left Thomas, she had accused him of
abusing those little girls and she brought them up to hate
him. It served her purpose at the time, but not when he got
rich, and none of it was true. Nor the rumour, also
implanted by her, that Thomas's father, the headmaster of
the school which once existed here, was just as bad.

She went back to typing. There was the faintest sound of someone else stirring in the house.

Two years after the night I burgled him, I came back. There was nowhere else to go. Thomas let me in, and I stayed as housekeeper. We rescued one another in our separate ways. He became my teacher and mentor, I his pupil and fellow collector. Thomas lived for paintings and the sea. It took him a year to tell me who was in the cellar and who had been there, that night. It took another year or so for me to fall in love with him, and then we were married for two years before he died. He left me everything: this house and all the paintings in it. It is a massive and important collection with a certain distinction. Most of the best paintings are anonymous.

His daughters were deliberately disenfranchised and they hated me. I can see their point but they would never have preserved anything, they would have destroyed it. Thomas knew that. He and Saul both knew that. I thought they might come to see him as he was.

Ten years to the day after I came in to find car keys, Gayle, Patrick's mother, and her husband came back to steal the most precious paintings, or so they thought. We set them up, to blackmail them. It worked and it also went wrong, because Gayle's hatred drove her mad and she almost killed me. I am sorry for

Gayle, because she had an epiphany that night, just as I had ten years before. She saw that her mother had lied, that her father had loved her and she saw what she had lost. She also saw ...

This is not succinct, Di told herself. There is no way to make a complicated story succinct. You mustn't include comment with reportage. If anyone wants to know the whole truth, they can go to Thomas's diaries. Gayle may do that, one day. Beatrice, her sister, probably not. Patrick knows the truth of his grandfather by instinct: he always did. They liked each other since the day they met, and nothing ever changed. Continue.

Well. Gayle and her husband think they were caught on camera beating the shit out of me and stealing things. That was enough to compromise any moral claim they may have had on Thomas's estate. And they got two valuable paintings, though not as valuable as they thought they were. They think that Saul and I have evidence enough to send them down. Gayle lets Patrick come back. Little do they know that I would never send anyone to prison. No one goes to prison on my watch.

They are safe from me. I, on the other hand, am not safe from them. Edward, Gayle's husband, and Beatrice are biding their time. And I can never let them know that their mother's bones are in the cellar. Still. Maybe Patrick, one day.

Saul came into the long room. The sun shone fitfully through grand windows and the hazy heat of yesterday was promising to return. Di's skin was as brown as light beer; she was indistinguishable from the shingle on the beach and it suited her. To his aesthetic eye, she was becoming so severely beautiful she should be painted herself. Not that she would know: she spent more time facing a computer screen than she did a mirror. She touched the surface of paint more obsessively than she did her own skin.

'At it again?' he said to her. 'Trying to explain the inexplicable by writing it down? Dearest Di, you must know by now that whatever you write, no one is going to believe you.'

'Except you.'

'We were the ones who knew Thomas best,' Saul said. 'Although I have to concede that a wife has superior knowledge over an agent and long-term friend, such as I.'

'We weren't in competition, Saul, still aren't. Would you call us soulmates?'

'Such a vulgar phrase, but yes, I suppose so. The same obsessive liquid running through our veins. Collaborators

25

with a common goal, united in reverence for Thomas Porteous and his purposes, something like that. It's just as well that I like you as much as I do, otherwise this endlessly forgiving nature of yours would irritate my bowels. You shouldn't have let Gayle back in, even for a second. Leopards don't change spots.'

She rose and walked round the room. The pictures on the walls greeted her: the swagger portrait of Madame de Belleroche and her cavalier on the opposite wall greeted one another. The best picture of all was the sea outside, murmuring away. How calm it was today. Di could see the pier in the near distance, with discernible figures walking on it, and longed to be there.

'Well, if a forgiving nature is all you have to criticise me for, I can't be doing so badly,' she said. 'Is there anything else? Such as me fiddling while Rome burns?'

'Something like that. You're out playing sandcastles, watching birds and learning to fish, instead of donning your glad rags and swooping down on the bargains in the art world. Never was a better time to buy. You've got to get out there and let it be known you're looking. Be a presence on the scene, go to the auctions, so that we get people to come to you. We've got to extend the collection before we put it on the map. We've got to do something about that glorious cellar, it's such a natural exhibition space. And you haven't even looked at the bloody bones.'

Saul was like the rest. He made no allowances for grief. The lassitude of it.

'I've been leaving it to you to do something about the bloody bones, and you haven't done a thing. You haven't even looked.'

Di winced. The bones of the late Christina Porteous lived behind the door in the wall dividing the front segment of the huge cellar from the back. The back section sloped away beneath a vaulted ceiling, blocked off by a wall and a door. Christina's door to Christina's self-appointed burial chamber, where she had lain in dry state for more than a decade.

'Jones looked a few weeks ago. Didn't he tell you?'

'Has he indeed? Good old Uncle Jones. Well, he was once a policeman, so nothing shocks. Is it dry down there? No floods for a long, long time.'

Saul spoke like the expert he was not, airily dismissing a problem which was thwarting his ambitions for the legacy of Thomas Porteous. In reality, he was squeamish, added to which, he had known Christina Porteous and loathed her memory. There was no sentiment attached to what happened to her bones, but there was a fear of contagion. Apart from Di, and one other, Saul had scant tolerance for women, anyway. Paintings were another matter: paintings and the exhibition thereof were Saul's sole passion, and the cellar was potentially glorious for the purpose.

'According to Jones,' Di said, 'you don't need smelling salts. Christina is bones and rags, cleaned by crabs, perhaps. And yes, I have seen, before we closed the door again. That much was my duty. If it wasn't for her, I might never have found Thomas and we might never have saved one another. So I owe her skeleton something better, and besides . . . '

'You owe her nothing, you don't owe anybody anything, you did two years in prison for saying nothing . . . you silly *woman*,' Saul yelled. 'Why can't we just put her in a bag and take it to the dump?'

Di moved towards the window. In the far distance, she could see waves crashing against an invisible barrier. She had, as Thomas remarked, and Saul appreciated, superb eyesight, as if she had binoculars already attached. He looked at her in infuriated admiration. These days, she had a peculiar dignity, and the squint when she looked closely at the surface of a picture was mere habit. She could *feel* a painting: she seemed to use all her sensory perceptions of touch, taste, smell when she looked at a canvas. If only she were interested in clothes, she could be a presence in the art world. Like everywhere else, clothes mattered; or maybe he had got that wrong, too.

'Thomas didn't want her taken to the tip. She tortured him in life, and she did after her death, but he did admire her single-mindedness. She always liked the idea of burial at sea. She hated and envied this house, but she loved being among the waves. She was perfectly clear about what she wanted to happen to her body after her death. He had a separate instruction for what should happen to her bones, based on that wish of hers.'

'Oh God,' Saul said. 'So he did. I hoped you'd forgotten. Burial at sea?'

'Burial in the sea.'

He moved towards the window. There was a telescope on a stand. Through that, he could see the thin line of foam in the distance.

'The Goodwin Sands,' Di said. 'She has to go to the Goodwin Sands.'

'Through those waves?' Saul said. 'They're seven miles away and I can see them. They must be a hundred feet high.'

'Only on a bad day. It can be calm.'

29

Silence fell. Saul was exasperated. She was stubborn and she was restless and she seemed to be terminally depressed unless she was out playing on the beach. This was dangerous to the enterprise. He needed her calm and focused on the collection.

Jones came in. He had given a perfunctory knock, turned on his heel and saluted. Jones had spent years as the local policeman, prematurely and involuntarily retired on account of his ambivalent and creative attitude to law and order. He was a cousin of Di's dead mother, a sworn enemy of her father, and he was intimately acquainted with the history of her life as well as the history of the house. His role in Di's life was something of which he was both proud and ashamed, because he had not looked out for her enough when she was a child: he had been instrumental in sending her to prison, and he had not quite made up for it since.

Basically, he looked after the house, and was protective of its occupants, especially Peg.

He knew about the bones. He knew they were down there, wrapped in purple, cursing them all.

'Did I hear mention of bones?' he said, breezily. Jones had a tendency to make light of the darkest subjects, not always appropriately. He was free of sentiment, a cynic and yet profoundly sentimental. 'Only there's another reason for clearing out the cellar, Di, love. Another reason other than his majesty,' a deferential nod to Saul, 'wanting to turn it into another fucking art gallery. The roof's getting dodgy. We'll need a bricklayer in there, sometime soon. Not that that's the only thing dodgy in this house.'

'Shall we do an inspection?' Saul said. 'It might be timely.'

'Yeah, fucking right,' Jones said.

'My dear Diana,' Saul said, extending his arm. 'Let us take a tour round the domain. It's high time you looked at it with a fresh eye.'

He meant that it might be timely to remind Diana Porteous of how much she had, rather than how much she had lost. Gained and lost, lost and gained, there must be a balance. She had gained a most remarkable man: she had acquired an education and a mission. She was the owner of a large house and a fantastic collection of pictures designed for a wider audience. She had acquired and finessed her fantastic eye for colour, shape, form, and she had lost the only person who seemed to have known her.

The house of Thomas Porteous had once been a fine

schoolhouse, built to high Victorian standards with a
lighter than average touch as an institutional building
designed to inspire the inhabitants with wide spaces, high,
coved ceilings and a lot else. Di allowed herself to be led
by two men with different purposes. Jones wanted to show
her the damp patches and the evidence of slipped tiles on
the roof, the need for rewiring, plumbing restoration and
the parlous state of the cellar. Saul wanted her to re-
examine and re-evaluate the sheer glory of the rooms and
the contents. He wanted her to get on with what she was
good at. She was a connoisseur. They went up to the top
floor, under the eaves, a room where a grown man could
stand easily in the middle although not at the sides.
Dormitories for children, comfortable spaces where you
could see convalescents or small persons curled up in iron
beds. It had been a hospital of sorts, temporarily. Small
pictures in here, miniatures on the walls and landings, big
colourful things of flowers on the facing walls. Too long
since Di had been up here. Then, down a floor, via the
stairs and the curving corridor, to the gallery room, once
a huge, part wood-panelled classroom with what might
have been the headmaster's study – an imposing room by
itself – off, with interconnecting doors that always stood
open. There were two sets of doors to every room, flanked

by the wavering corridor, and from there on down, two sets of stairs: one no doubt for servants, but adequate enough; the other, wider flight for those making an entrance or a rowdy exit. Di could hear feet clattering down those broader, wooden stairs, despite the worn carpet, and at the same time, she could imagine the more deferential footsteps coming up the other. She was aware of both men watching her, as if she was a cripple about to fall down or a little old lady reminded of the responsibilities of her vast inheritance. Saul, noticing that she paused before each painting, found himself immensely reassured. She had, after all, assisted Thomas in his latter acquisitions. The most marvellous thing about this collection, she reflected to herself, is that it contains the minimum of mistakes insofar as each painting shone with its own quality. It really did not matter if you did not know who painted what. She could feel the old enthusiasm returning, like an intermittent signal, bright, but interrupted.

It was time for Di to make her own mistakes, although it might take more than that to bring her alive.

'And as for the bathrooms,' Jones said, darkly, shaking his head. 'Oh my fucking dear. Plumbing sounds like a battle.'

He flushed a chain in the fifth lavatory to prove a point. The sound was like an enemy invasion.

'Drawings,' Di was saying. 'We need more black and white sketches, work in progress. We could have a room full of paintings by children. And as for the collection, we need more. Shit.'

She turned to Saul, urgently, lost for words, but with some of her old fire back.

'Things by living artists with traditional values,' she said. 'I mean people who paint, with real discipline, skill. Not only paintings by people already dead.'

'You want to have art classes here,' Jones said. 'People making stuff. If that's the way, cellar's the best place.'

They were back in the snug, next to the kitchen, where a big, friendly, fat-thighed nude hung opposite the blue chair where Thomas had sat when he died. Even that was not a small room, simply small by the standards of the bigger rooms in the place. There was room for them all to sink into comfortable chairs. It was shabby chic before it was invented; in other words, colourful-shabby, with pieces of furniture that seemed to have a life of their own, even if every damn thing needed to be resprung. In the kitchen, offstage, Peg was talking to the cooker. Come on, she was saying to it, do your thing. Peg whistled as she worked.

Pleased with herself. Going out, later. Peg had a life of her own.

Saul looked at Di, and Jones looked at Di, and the men nodded to one another and Di looked at no one. She had curled up into Thomas's chair, the blue one, and fallen fast asleep. Up at five, asleep by nine. She did a lot of that, these days.

'About thirty thousand for repairs, I reckon,' Jones said, talking over her head towards Saul. 'And that's the basics. Will she do it?'

'She's got to do something. For the safety of the pictures. And she's got to get out into the world,' Saul said. 'So what's this hanging around got to do with anything? Grief?'

Saul did not know about grief, or not as other people did. Grief was about lost opportunities. He had grieved for dead Thomas, but that was his own business. Jones was irritated.

'Yes, she'll pay for repairs, if only you can get the right builder, of course she will. A trusted person, hey? But in the meantime, what worries me is this. She's going to fall for the first bloke with a big dick who comes through the door. She's only twenty-eight, for God's sake. Remarkably mature, but she's gotta have hormones. You know what hormones are like, Saul. You can have a whole fucking orchestra working well, and then one little bolshie in the piccolo section screws the whole thing.'

'You do talk shit, Jones, you really do. Get to the point. Anytime now, she's gonna come through that door, on fire with a painting she's seen online, right back in the buying business.'

'But all the same, there's other things she's gotta do. She's got to do a bit more than being a fucking curator. I mean, there's life through the eyes, and then there's fucking life, see what I mean?'

'You mean she might want something else?' Saul said, puzzled.

'Yes, that's exactly what I mean. What I mean is fucking fucking. That's what she hasn't done enough of. No drinks, drugs 'n' rock 'n' roll either. No fucking fun.'

'But this *is* fun,' Saul said. 'Collecting and looking after paintings is the only real fun there is.'

'What fucking planet are you on?' Jones yelled. 'Fucking Mars? There's other things in life, you know. Ain't you ever been in love, Saul? Never been young, never been on fire with bloody lust?'

Saul shuddered.

'Not in a very long time. And since the last time I felt

those primeval urges it was for someone old and fat, it's just as well. Such things have been rightly eradicated from my being. I live for aesthetic enjoyment only. Thank your stars for that.'

'Well, I don't think they've been eradicated from Di. Nor do I think they'll have been eradicated from any full-blooded male who sees her. She's a knockout, Saul, or haven't you noticed?'

'Yes of course I have,' Saul said, smoothing his hair. 'She's thoroughly paintable, almost Pre-Raphaelite, such lovely bones, although I do think she's an acquired taste. And I rather hoped that she'd be able to resist that going sexually wild business, or at least for a while. And the drugs and rock and roll. Such a stupid, conventional path for a young heiress, been done so many times before, don't you think? So *fucking* boring. I thought we might find another challenge to bring her alive. Like exercising her original vocation.'

'What? Thieving?'

Di was half listening, half interested. She had no instinct to go wild, whatever that was. Maybe she was deficient. She'd done being bad; she'd been a pushover orphan who ran with a gang of thieves before going to prison and if that was running wild, it was distinctly overrated. The intense, quiet and tranquil excitement of life and learning with Thomas had been infinitely preferable. It was child-hood she wanted back, not the miseries of adolescence. Too late, she told herself, you are bound by a thousand responsibilities. And you are a collector.

All the same, she had to admit, yes, there were other things in life.

'Jones,' she said, startling them both, 'how do we take Christina's bones to the Goodwin Sands without anyone knowing?'

'Ask your bloody father,' Jones growled. 'He's the one who'd know about that.'

She turned to Saul.

'And what other project did you have in mind for me? What are you cooking up to bring me back to life?'

'A little in-depth, seriously intellectual research,' Saul said.

Jones groaned.

'To which end,' Saul said, 'I hope you don't mind, but you'll be getting a visitor tomorrow. I think you'll find her interesting. She wants to consult your expertise. And, again I hope you don't mind, but she'll come along with my sister. Sarah.'

His voice dropped a cadence as he mentioned the

name, Sarah, as if he was genuflecting towards it. Embracing it with reverence.

'A *sister*?' Jones said. 'A sister? You, with a real life sister? Some female influence on your life then? There's a turn up, if you like. Where does she live, then? Older, younger, all that shit? You're making it up, go on, you fucking are, you're pulling the wool.'

'Do shut up, you fucking philistine. I have mentioned her before, but I've been slow to introduce her. I might lie through my perfect teeth, sometimes, but I wouldn't ever lie about my sister Sarah, on account of the fact that she's the only woman on the whole planet I respect, apart from this woman here,' he said, dismissively, gesturing towards Di. 'And then only sometimes.'

'Thanks,' Di said.

'So what does she do, this fucking sister of yours, and why is she near by, and is she older or younger than you are, or fucking what?'

'Considerably younger, if you lop off a decade. Forty-something and in her prime,' Saul said, proudly, adding, 'She's got the best dress sense of anyone I know. Apart from me. And she lives two miles away.'

He shrugged with suspicious carelessness.

'Anyway, tea, tomorrow. My sister Sarah and her friend

Granta, who is, apparently, as old as the hills. Granta has been the victim of theft. Art theft.'

'I'm not turning up to no tea party,' Jones said, shuddering at the thought.

'Nobody asked you,' Saul said. 'You're the man of the sea. Perhaps you would like to investigate the little matter of how to remove bones from here to the fucking Goodwin Sands. All right with you?'

CHAPTER THREE

That was what they ought to have painted, instead of all those great big skies. They should have painted the huge yellow diggers reconfiguring the beach on the seafront of the town two weeks ago. Those big machines, he'd have liked a picture of that. A grey, warm day, where research was better done in the pub by the pier. Jones did not particularly want to do it, but always better out of the house.

He stood on the pier which was his second home and raised his binoculars to his eyes, imagined what the man would say. He scouted the horizon for a sight of Di's father, too. Fucking Quig.

Fucking Goodwin Sands.

If you want to go to the Goodwin Sands by boat, his man, Daniel, said, the wind and the tide had to be right. Wouldn't take anyone otherwise. Seven miles out, the Sands rose to the surface when the tides were low: not rising, simply existing. On rough days, the sea rebelled from beneath against the subversive presence of the subversive Sands, rearing up against them in waves a hundred feet high, great plumes of biblical proportions, impossible to navigate, as if the sea was trying to destroy the freakish obstacle by battering it to death. The Sands were never destroyed: they merely shifted, changed shape and contour, so that when they were visible again, they were never quite the same, but still there; the mild, hidden mountain range under the sea, the remnants of an island. Jones approved of them in principle: he liked the anarchic, even if he was afraid.

And these damn fools, them with the diggers on the far side of the pier, thought they could change the shape of things? Chuck up a few thousand tons of shingle and sand and imagine it would make any difference? If the fucking Sands, seven miles out there, had refused to change in a few years, why should anything else?

Still, Jones had to listen. Not only did he want to know, and was ashamed of his ignorance, but hell, it was something to do. He was hurt by this errand, as if he was good for nothing else. Still, it could come in useful. He could tell it all to Patrick another time, ham it up.

The Goodwins trapped the unwary as well as the wary: there were hundreds of wrecks and bodies buried deep there. The screams of the drowning could be heard from land. Vessels of every kind and size had foundered on these sands, been driven against the unyielding mass by wind and tide and blundered into the trap. A graveyard of ships, a burial ground in layers. Scenes of mayhem and murder, smugglers robbing wrecks. And yet, perversely, the same hidden mountain range made a wall between the wildness beyond, leaving relatively calmer waters between themselves and the shore. 'A sheltering place, see?' Daniel said. 'Nelson parked his fleet here.' Cargo boats, container ships, ferries, marooned vessels sought the same protection. Ship watchers watched them from shore. People tracked progress and identities on iPhone apps.

'And then they had another life,' Daniel explained on his second pint. 'For treasure seekers and picnickers on the few days in summer when you could get out there. People played cricket. Short games, though. Something to say you'd done, you know? You never leave a trace. Footprints fill with water as you watch: you can't leave a mark on the place. Land of a sort, borrowed land, not dry land. Loneliest place on earth.'

A poet, Jones thought, trying to remember if he had ever arrested him for anything. Daniel and his mate still took people out to the Sands. Ten, no more, in the old fishing boat. Daniel took able-bodied explorers, beachcombers and persons with binoculars, those who wanted to scatter ashes at sea. An hour and half max to explore after they got off the tender he carried behind the boat. Plenty of time to say your prayers, collect your souvenirs, gawk at the resident seals if they were obliging enough to appear, and not walk too far. That was the danger in taking people to the Sands, this small window of time; because once they were on there, they forgot where they were and time seemed irrelevant. Perched on the edge where they landed, they looked at this vast expanse of smooth-surfaced wilderness, any colour from sepia to gold, then they looked for a speck in the distance and walked towards it, encountering, instead of smoothness, shallow valleys and hills, clear water pools and soft, heavy mud. The light, refracted from the pools, the ripples on the sand, mesmerised the people who walked too far, beckoned by the mirage of a horizon, went down the dips and forgot all sense of time.

'Then,' Daniel said, 'I'm fucked and I scream at them, because if they don't get back to the tender on time, I'm going to have to leave them.'

Some people went to bury things.

'Can't stand those folk who want a spiritual experience,' he told Jones. 'You know, the dreamer who goes off on one, forgets how long he's walked and has no idea how long it might take to walk back, thinking he's going to go back the same way and follow his own footprints. You can't, they've gone, they've gone and the world's deaf out there.'

Daniel put down his drink and shivered.

'I sweat it out, cos if four come back, and the last one doesn't, I know I've got to leave him and go. No more can I go looking for him, either.'

'You'd leave him to die?'

'I'd leave him to the coastguard, and hope he wouldn't die, but yes, I'd leave him.'

'Happened yet?'

'No, not yet, but close. I have nightmares about it, but gotta earn a living, hey?'

Jones bought him another pint, always amazed by his town and the people in it. Only ever known the half of it. He had never set foot on those damn Sands. Who would want to be buried there, unless someone wanting the company of other bones? It made him angry that anyone should listen to the selfish wish of a selfish woman to be consigned to the sea in a dangerous way that might take someone down with her. A malicious instruction. And Di: Di in her present state, she'd be the one who'd go wandering off, not caring if she came back. Jones walked back towards Di's place, wondering if he'd had a drink or two with the last honourable man on the planet. Di's place? When he had first known it, it was where he went to school. Jones could read and write because of this place.

He slammed the door behind him as he went in. Jones had a room at the top of the house, whenever he wanted it. Peg had a room below: this was a place of many rooms where people could come and go privately and its history included a dedication to education which somehow gave it a certain tranquillity at odds with the sea beyond. The talk of the Sands disturbed him.

He went up to the top of the house. En route up the back stairs, past the gallery room with the ever-open doors, he could swear he could hear the tinkle of teacups and spoons. Peeking in, unseen, he saw a glimpse of a very old woman sitting upright in the best chair. And he heard the melodious voice of a younger woman who sounded like Saul. Jones cheered up. Plots afoot, and new friends, hey? Di needed these and she needed something. He hoped to God they liked each other. Because if she got distracted by new stuff, she would forget about the Good-win Sands.

An awkward grouping: the old woman who looked like an ogre, her apparent acolyte and Di, the fierce girl with the bad hair who was not used to socialising. Since the death of Thomas over a year ago, many had desired to make the acquaintance of Mrs Porteous, Mark Two, suspicious scrubber that she was, and they had always found her to be out or busy. Fact was, as Saul knew very well, Mrs Diana Porteous was a connoisseur of paintings, the chatelaine of a big house, familiar with art history, not unfamiliar with fine food, and with an innate, exquisite good taste while, at the same time, she was also a creature with few social graces. She could restore a canvas, she could design, she could write in sentences; she was a grad-uate in her own right, but she had been reclusive with Thomas and his founts of wisdom and she had never been a normal child or teenager going through all those rites of passage, unless you counted two years in prison. All right, Thomas had been civilised to his very core, and a certain amount rubbed off, like his use of language, but Di still didn't know how to adapt to different companies. Such as when to speak up, and when to pipe down, how not to make it plain in every word and gesture that she did not like whoever it was. Lacking in diplomacy, was how Saul put it.

His sister, Sarah, on the other hand, was a complete chameleon: she could change her colours and her spots to suit any occasion and she was charm personified. The right sort of charm, based on insatiable curiosity. Saul's sister, the only woman he truly loved, had suspended conventional judgements long ago in favour of her own version of morality. However sophisticated she was, she would always be an outsider.

Sarah was dressed in a brown linen skirt, with a touch of mud at the hem, a cream linen shirt with artful pleats, and training shoes that had seen better days. Her ears and hands wore tiny rings. She looked like a stylish gypsy who had just romped over the hill. Saul himself was a study in grey and white, decidedly nervous. A great deal hung on this meeting.

The old lady in the other chair looked blank. Di looked ferocious. She felt she was being outmanoeuvred and was getting ready to dig her heels into the carpet, although her instinct was to like Sarah on sight, if only because she envied the insouciance of her clothes. She had been longing for another woman in her life. Peg was great, but Peg was a child.

Sarah was not old, early forties perhaps, with the gamine grace of a small colt and the straight-backed deportment of a dancer. She had a seductive air of sheer mischief. The old woman spoke and when she smiled, her face became a jungle of lines, suddenly appealing and almost clownish.

'Ah,' she said, 'how this place has changed for the better. You must have breathed life into it, my dear, just as you breathed life into old Thomas. You must miss him terribly. Being widowed is absolutely bloody, isn't it?'

'You've been here before?' Di asked, surprised. No one had warned her about this. This vivid old lady with the rough voice had never crossed the threshold as long as she had lived here.

'Oh yes, many times. Must be fifteen years, though. We were friends, Thomas and I. I liked Thomas very much indeed. Tell me, when is it you miss him most?'

The question was impertinent, but the implicit fellow feeling of widowhood and loss rose to the surface, cutting across the vast difference in their ages and Granta's gimlet glare. It made Di respond.

'I miss him all the time. I miss him whenever I have to make a decision. I miss him when I go to sleep and when I wake up,' Di said.

'Good. Better than bitterness. Just thank your good luck he died, rather than left you. I wish mine had died.'

'I thought you said he had.'

'Yes he did, but he left me first. I'd rather it was the other way round.' She leant forward, large in her seat, eyes bright.

'I believe Thomas's father and my husband had the same cleaning lady at one point. My husband was an awful, manipulative shit and I hated him. Not like your Thomas. He was wonderful. He liked our paintings – my husband sold him one or two of his, I think. Ones he didn't like because he didn't know who painted them. I wonder if my husband liked him because he was rich, like we were? I really liked Thomas.'

'So why didn't you come and see him, then? If you liked him, and you were friends, why didn't you come and see him? Why did everyone leave him alone?'

Di was angry. Granta raised her arms in self-defence.

'I can't speak for anyone else. Or the rumours. I only know I didn't because I became a bitter and twisted old bitch, got stuck in that groove. I wallowed in malicious self-pity. Miss Haversham eating her own bile, stayed like that for years. I did a good job of it, didn't I, dear?'

She turned to Sarah.

'You surely did,' Sarah said cheerfully. 'You were perfectly, hideously foul.' She turned to Di. 'Granta was my landlady when I first came to the village, and she still is. We're only two miles away, if you go by the beach. She owns half of it. Vicious old brute, she was, and she's not terribly nice now. Yes, dear, you were a monster. Nobody asked you to tea, and if they did you'd stick the knife in.'

Granta pulled a face at her.

'Then Sarah arrived,' she said. 'Sarah has the knack of persisting with the unlikeable and the uneatable, like me. You keep telling her to bugger off and she kept on coming back. These days I'm almost human, but don't be fooled. Do you like my dress?'

The dress was an immense tent of black and cream stripes which folded around her and could have served equally well as curtains. Granta sighed, fingered the cloth round her knees, looking round the room at the same time.

'You know, Mrs Porteous, the paintings in here are bloody marvellous. We used to come here for drinks. Always loved Madame de Belleroche. And that one, on the other side. Looks as if he's paying court.' She pointed at the painting. 'Thank God you kept Thomas alive, my dear.'

Di could feel her own smile, spreading across her face. Granta leant forward, sipped tea decorously, putting it down with disdain.

'I don't suppose you've got any gin, have you?'

'Of course,' Di said. 'Dutch or English?'

Granta beamed. 'The Dutch variety's made to go with tea. What a good girl you are. A veritable girl with a pearl earring. Thomas was right about you. Do you know how much he loved you?'

From his seat in the corner, Saul began to breathe. Touch and go, so far, and now it was light touchpaper and retire. He was preparing to sidle out of the room via the second staircase when Granta noticed and poked a varnished fingernail wearily towards the ceiling. She had pretty hands and small, nurtured feet.

'Sarah, love, tell that little shit to stay still. It was his idea, after all.'

'What was?' Di said, quietly and, to Sarah's ears, ominously.

'This meeting, of course,' Granta said, speaking directly to Di.

'Why?' Di said.

'Oh, for God's sake, didn't anybody tell you? This meeting's been engineered because I need your help and by the look of you, you need Sarah's. You look like something the cat brought in.'

Di found herself liking the fact that Granta was so rude. It was stimulating.

'So what kind of help can you possibly want from me?'

The varnished hands fluttered.

'Your expertise in paintings, my dear. Of course.'

Sarah interrupted. 'What she really means is that she wishes to consult your expertise as a thief. Or, let's say, a recoverer of things.'

Silence fell. The suggestion could have been insulting but, strangely, wasn't. Di didn't even mind that they knew her history and she had forgotten all about the bones in the cellar in a pleasant rushing of blood to the head. The sun woke up and streamed through the window next to her, bringing the promise of the fine evening which had been denied all day. Leaning against the glass, she could see the long line of the Goodwin Sands.

'I'm an out-of-date thief,' she said. 'And theft is always wrong,' she added, sounding prim.

'Not always,' Granta said. 'Not if the stuff's been stolen from you already. By your own son.'

'You know what you are?' Sarah said to Granta. 'You're a wicked old bitch.'

'But does she tell the truth?' Saul asked.

'Oh yes. Not always, and when she does, she doesn't always dress it up in its best clothes.'

She beamed at Di, and Di beamed back.

CHAPTER FOUR

Picture. *The beach in Deauville, circa 1936.*
Lounge lizards in bathing suits, under a parasol.
Helen McKie.

'So that's the story. Do you believe it?' Sarah said.

Sarah and Di sat on the shingle beach, listening to the waves. Granta had summoned a taxi home to the village two miles down the coast by foot, three by road, where she lived in the lee of the cliffs at the foot of a valley clawed out of chalk. Not like this flatness where you could see for ever with the cliffs rising only in the distance.

'Why shouldn't I believe it? I like Granta.'

'And you tend to believe people you like?'

'Yes. Just as I believe you because I like you.'

'Thank you for that,' Sarah said. 'The feeling's entirely mutual, believe me.'

They did not touch; no shaking of hands. There was no need.

'And you don't mind that Saul engineered this?'

'No. I believe in happenstance. It's served me well. And I believe in Saul, his motives, at least.'

Sarah grinned.

'About Granta,' she said, returning to the story. 'It was Granta's husband Henry who courted Thomas first, after Thomas moved back to the schoolhouse. Henry built the sprawl of houses at the back of our village and bagged a big old house at the front. He was the kind of rich man who could never have enough. He acquired everything and anything that could be acquired. Houses, boats, streets and still no one gave him the respect he wanted. Scatter-gun taste, that was him. He hoovered up possessions, went for glitter rather than gold, no taste. Which was why he envied Thomas, who had. Enough of Granta's story. It's better the way she tells it, even with all the holes. Anyway, he left and died. Left Granta enough but nothing for his son. Son came back and stole Granta's paintings, says they were his.

'Look, look,' she cried. 'There's the moon, oh glory be, what a sight. Let's wish on the old moon.'

A rare, balmy night on this coast, growing chillier. Di's initial, angry reaction to the realisation that Saul had told Sarah every single detail he knew about her past and present, faded from being a betrayal to being a relief. It meant she had nothing to hide or explain. Di was having a moment of happiness, sitting on a dark beach with a woman who talked so directly and was also willing to accept the silences. *Real friends,* Thomas said, *are those to whom you can tell everything, and also those who respect your secrets.* And yes, friendship could be instant, like love.

'Anyway,' Sarah said. 'You know what a plotter my brother is.'

'Yes. I know.'

'And you don't resent it?'

'No, not now.'

The moon appeared, larger, rising like half-baked cake, already nibbled by mouthy clouds. Sarah started to laugh.

'Men,' she said. 'Why are they such plotters and planners? Why's life never enough for them and why do they never have enough?'

57

'Must be the constant desire to rule the world,' Di said. 'And what is it that Saul's plotting for both of us?'

'He wants you to acquire some of my sophistications,' Sarah said, mimicking Saul's slightly high voice. 'He wants you to be able to stalk through the world in good clothes exerting your authority. He wants you to acquire – oh, how did he put it? – "a veneer of confidence". Just like me.'

They both began to giggle.

'You can see,' Sarah said, scraping the shingle with her muddy shoe, 'that I know my brother better than he knows me. But I am good at *veneers* and I adore dressing up.'

'And there was I thinking he wanted me to go back to being a thief,' Di said.

'That, too, probably, in a manner of speaking,' Sarah said, mimicking him again. 'You know that Saul was an accomplished burglar once, but only for the right cause.'

'So was I,' Di sighed. 'And not for any cause. I was good at getting into places when I was a girl, you see. A little worm, that was me. And the best ever thrower of stones. Don't tell me that's what Saul wants me to do. I can't ever do it again, even though,' she said, wistfully, her voice trailing off, 'thieving was the best fun, sometimes, until I was sent in to Thomas and knew it was all wrong.

You mustn't steal what someone has tried to preserve. But I was an excellent thrower of stones.'

Sarah watched as Di flung a stone into the sea. It landed far, far out with an audible sound as if it was dead on some invisible target. She threw another: it seemed to Sarah as if it had hit exactly the same spot before the other had finally submerged. The movement of her arms were as fluid as the water. Sarah would not have wanted her as an enemy. With an aim like that she could have taken on Goliath.

'We used to swim and set floats,' Di said. 'Targets in the water. Have stone-throwing competitions. We'd swim out and lay a line of cans, bottles, strung out. I learned to win. It was the one thing where I was better than anyone else. That's how the thieving thing started. I could smash a window from any distance, even a tiny little window. Do that, one night, come back another night if nobody noticed. Go up the wall. Not a day goes by when I don't throw a stone.'

'Saul won't want you to do that,' Sarah said.

The sea slurred.

'Possibly a bit more subtle,' Sarah went on. 'He wants you to set flares against the young thief who stole Granta's paintings. He thinks it might bring you alive. Granta thought it would be a good idea for me to go and seduce the thief, but I'm just a little bit too old for seduction. Anyway, if Granta gets her paintings back, she'll give them to the Porteous collection. *Voilà*, several birds with several stones. Saul increases the collection; you learn the arts of persuasion and exercise your alternative skills. As a preliminary, we go shopping.'

'They must be good pictures.'

'Some of them must be. I don't know. I only know the size of the stolen ones because of the gaps on Granta's walls. Saul's become obsessively interested in S. Cockerel. He's one of those hedge-fund-manager types, turned art collector. Maybe just like his father. The paintings must be valuable, why else take them away?'

'Value isn't the point.'

'Might be the entire point. Do you know, Saul does over-complicate things. He might just want you to target the man, get in there and see what there is.'

Di laughed. 'Dressed in my new best clothes?'

'Of course. Clothes are important for any enterprise. So when are we going shopping?'

Sarah plucked the smallest round stone she could find and threw it, watching it land not far from her own feet, not even reaching the sea. All her strength was in her legs while Di's was in her arms. Di watched the moon rise and shine like a pale fire. The night was still young. She had forgotten everything else but Granta's story and Sarah's presence. A son stealing from his mother, not nice. At least Gayle and Edward had waited until Thomas was dead. There was the old stirring of excitement, the feeling of going hunting. And the thought of going shopping with Sarah was pretty damn good.

'Saul wants you as flag bearer for the collection. For that you need dressage, how to look, how to sidestep, how to be convincing. I'm not so sure, but that's where I come in. I've been fooling most of the people most of the time for most of my life and I know how to dress as if I didn't care. And,' she paused to drain her glass and upturn it on the stones, 'I'm a city person. Those rich London streets are my old hunting ground.'

'If I understand this right,' Di said, carefully, 'I'm being given a challenge to bring me alive and stop me going off the rails?'

'To remind you of the other aspects of yourself, perhaps. Dear Saul also wants you to travel. You might have seen half the major paintings of the world online, but it's a different thing to see them where they live. I'm game for all that, if you are.'

'Thomas used to say you can see the whole world from your doorstep.'

'Especially now. You've got virtual reality on a screen, but it isn't quite the same. You have to make real journeys. After all, Thomas knew the big wide world before he rejected it. You don't.'

It was gently said. Di accepted it.

'Steven Cockerel, who stole Granta's paintings? Did she love him?'

'Oh yes,' Sarah said. 'He's her son. She loved him intensely, still does.'

'That makes a difference,' Di said. 'Let's go shopping. I would really, really like to do that.'

'Well?' Saul said when Di came indoors, glowing. 'What do you think of my glorious sister? Have you drowned her? Personally, I consider her certifiably insane and totally unafraid of the dark side. What do you think? Did she romp back over the cliffs to that ghastly, twee village?'

'I think drowning's too good for you, Saul. But whatever the plan was, it worked. I'll go up to London with Sarah and shop till I drop. Tell me about this thief and these paintings and why you want them.'

'They might, just might, be glorious seascapes. Are we

sitting comfortably?' he said, gesturing towards his laptop screen. 'I've boiled it down to a few lines.

Steven Cockerel, entrepreneur, self-made materialist. No class but plenty of dosh. A man who understands the essential rules of capitalism, which is buy cheap, sell dear. Take no prisoners and go easy on the sentiment.

Graduated in geography from Cambridge. Augmented undergraduate income by selling fish and floated his first company at twenty-two. Thereafter, went into buying and selling whatever there was to buy and sell. Aged thirty-five. Estranged from father who had paid for public school education and disapproved of the result. Cockerel senior, property developer, likewise highly acquisitive, dies, leaves widow, Granta Cockerel, as sole heir. Disgruntled son makes up to grieving widow/stepmother and relieves her of valuable paintings.'

'Who wrote this?' Di said. 'Where's the facts? It isn't a report, it's just a series of impressions.'

'Distilled, I assure you, from hours of online to-be-continued research, and my own inimitable conclusions. We are, of course, on familiar ground when it comes to dealing with the children of rich fathers. The fury of disenfranchisement turning them into thieves.'

'But you don't *know* that, Saul. Supposing he was

entitled to them? Supposing Granta gave them away? Suppose there was a will, left them to him.'

'The will's a matter of public record, and it doesn't say so. And according to Granta, he threatened to burn her house down. Even allowing for exaggeration, she didn't part with them voluntarily.'

He yawned.

'Sleep on it, lovely. I'm so glad you like my sister. You're going to have so much fun doing retail with her.'

'And what are we shopping for?' Di asked, laughing despite herself.

'Life,' Saul said. 'Style. Panache.'

'Where does the thief live?'

'Ah yes. A rather special place, you might take a look at that when you're up in the Smoke. He's the worst kind of collector. He collects paintings and stores them away to sell at a profit. Probably sits in state, gloating. It's not about preserving or enjoying, it's about getting richer.'

Diana Porteous was unconvinced, but still, she slept happier than she had for a year, oblivious to the sounds of the house, which breathed in and out with steady, peaceful sea sounds.

She had forgotten to listen out for Peg, but then again, Peg seemed to prefer that she didn't. Let the girl alone.

Upstairs, Peg, de facto housekeeper, bloody good at all that, dozed in the smallest bedroom in the house, which suited her best. The size of the place was alarming when Jones wasn't around. A refugee from London, rescued by Di when fare-dodging on the train from here to there, and later from worse, she loved it here, and she bloody loved working here and learning stuff. Following in Di's footsteps, she was, although the imprint of those steps was rather too large. She was paying her debts, but she wasn't going to stay here for ever, no way. Jones said, the sky's the limit, Peg love, learn to drive, learn to cook, master the iPhone and the world's your fucking oyster. And when you've got that fucking diploma in hairstyling, well, you can sail away on a whale.

It was Jones got her the iPhone, and she loved it. She loved Jones, simply loved him. She loved Di, too, with a reserved, critical devotion, which meant she could never say so, any more than it was demanded of her to show either gratitude or affection. She halfway wished it was, so she could rebel against it and say 'So? I work hard, don't I? Whadya want? You're not my mother.' She wanted to be resentful but wasn't allowed; everything she did was appreciated. Christ, she was nineteen, in the best care home she could ever have got, with the best training she could ever have wanted, and she knew who she owed for the chance. Peg sighed, this time with satisfaction. She was well on her way to paying her debts, she really was, with a bit more to go. It freed up the mind for stuff.

One of the problems about here was that she was more than a little afraid of the sea. Until she got the iPhone. Marinetraffic.com was a blast, put the whole thing into perspective. You could see what was going on out at sea without going anywhere nearer, didn't even have to put your feet in. Maybe she was just afraid of the dogs on the beach; they scared her much more than people. She had a scar on her arm from a bite.

Even at night, she could check the boats she saw on the horizon in this busy stretch of water, and that was magic. Before that, it had been threatening. Now she could see the shape of a big boat in the distance, way beyond the Goodwin Sands, lit at night or glinting in the morning sun, and she could find out who it was. *Miss Miranda, sailing from Argentina, bound for Portsmouth.* Or follow the next, squat shape of a dredger out of port, tugging away east, following a zigzag line on the screen, like the one she had seen with Patrick, towing away the mile of pipe that had pumped all that shingle ashore to plump up the beach a mile away. A bigger shape of boat, explained, you could even call up a picture of it. *Tringaling en route to Rotterdam. Minerva from Singapore.*

They kept trying to get her to read, but really, she would rather listen and watch, and do. And she slept quietly on this calm night, nursing a text from a boy in the town.

She wanted everything shipshape before she went, wanted everyone to be friends. And they were all a bit stupid, really, except Patrick. But she did love Jones.

PART TWO

CHAPTER FIVE

Picture. *A portrait of a City businessman, probably commissioned circa 1910. The man with a high wing collar, a fine head of hair and a stupendous moustache, sitting on a grand chair, complete with top hat. The magnate depicted as a kind of pope, half smiling, a fount of wisdom and benevolence, about to distribute blessings. The cold eyes and ruddy skin contrast with the vivid royal purple of his cravat. The background is anonymous, lacking a throne.*

These days, Steven Cockerel thought, the vestments of secular power were not the same and it was not easy to dress for the part. The clergy had the best of it. In the second decade of the twenty-first century, the nobles of the business world had so little opportunity to show off. Flamboyance, even of the kind in the portrait, was definitely out. Steven examined the man in the painting. Everything about him screamed riches. The clothes were complicated and required the help of a valet as well as another servant to launder his perfect linen. The dull gold of the watch chain glittered. His boots were high-polished perfection and would have required assistance in the lacing. This man did not bend to tie his own shoes. He rested his hands on his knees; the artist no doubt bowing before him, ready to help him from the chair.

Steven looked at the plutocrat and wondered about the artist. What was he paid, for instance, or if he was ever paid. Steven could kid himself that he had bought the thing for its quality, but really he had acquired it to give himself a role model. He had wanted to look as rich and powerful as this man did: the sort of man who commanded silence and obedience by his very appearance. That was denied to Steven. How *did* a man show his wealth these days? The designer watch? The easy-to-wear designer suit? The right kind of car that could never be left unattended? How did a person of wealth make it clear what they were when they could not even wear a top hat in lieu of a crown? Or carry a silver-topped cane from Asprey's? It puzzled Steven that, rich as he was, he was forced to look just the same as everyone else. There was nothing he could do to underline his own distinctions.

Nor, on the other hand, could *he* have the same beliefs as the man in the painting. That bloody man in the portrait knew his status was going to last for ever, while Steven had no such illusions. The man mocked him. Steven retreated back a few steps to the other side of the room where the dartboard was, picked up the darts and threw them towards the canvas. Bingo. Two darts landed in the hat and now the man looked ridiculous. The darts landed with a mild thwumping sound that made Steven laugh. Not for the first time, he was uncomfortably aware that he was not a nice man. Who cared? It was his painting; it was worth nothing: he could do what he liked with it.

Oh, for a Jeeves or a similar butler to dress him in this style and guide him, although he scarcely needed a Jeeves in this place. Two cleaning women came in once a week from an agency. They removed dust and what little grime he left since he was assiduous about cleaning up after himself. The chambers he had gutted to create this mini-malist paradise had white floors, grey walls, white and black kitchen, and acres of wall space. No one could look in on this fifth-floor height unless they had wings, but then again, no more could he look out, which he scarcely did anyway, except sometimes when he picked up a precious object to examine it in the light and remind it that it was a long way down to the hard surface of the road below should he choose to throw it away. The flat was insulated for sound. The fact that he lived in a con-version made out of the old, upstairs chambers in a decommissioned Victorian bank, pleased him mightily. Ironic, yes.

Footsteps. A door opening.

'Meester Cokrill. Is OK we clean now?'

'Yes, fine. Thank you.'

A flash of blind irritation. He could not stay here a moment longer and listen to the very sound of someone cleaning up his minimal mess. The noise of a vacuum cleaner was repellent. Besides, there were other worlds to conquer outside here. He was going to cover these walls and earn his next million in the way he had already begun.

He threw the last dart and impaled the man in the

picture through his nose. Really, he was not a nice man. But nicer than the man he was going to meet. Old schoolchum Edward, who couldn't even pretend to be nice, and who had a picture to sell.

Steven Cockerel, who had always despised his name, closed the door of his flat behind himself. It clicked shut with the quiet efficiency of a heavy oak door. He skipped across the landing down one mean flight of steps, reached the next floor and paused to lean over the balustrade, looking down into the grand, oak-lined vestibule below. Light poured through huge windows, revealing the acres of old oak panelling which covered the walls. There was a carved porch above the old revolving door. The chandeliers, prescribed decoration for a grand banking hall, still hung there, listlessly. There was a smattering of carved chairs, marshalled against the walls. Really, the bank had screwed up big-time with this. The first two floors and this vestibule were up for lease, had been for a year, but the proposed rent was monstrous, and the restrictions on use so complex that even the most enthusiastic applicants had quailed after their initial investigations. It had its own severe beauty, but it was listed to within an inch of its elegant life. No leaseholder – ideally a gallery or an institution – would ever be allowed to do anything with it. No one could even stick a pin in a wall: whoever used it could never make it their own or change a single item. All permissions for planning consent had been refused. That might not be the case for ever, but it was the case for now. As it was, Steven and another tenant, who was absent, had somehow acquired the run of the whole building, which gave him perverse pleasure. He loved it when a bank screwed up so mightily. They'd accepted offers on the top two floors, effectively the ugly, modernised quarters, and then got stuck with the rest. All it was suitable for was an art installation, or a restaurant, and they weren't having anything to do with food.

So he was king of his castle, leaving him to rule it with the help of a ridiculously ineffectual security guard, who came in and patrolled the place at regular intervals and was called Janek.

Janek was there as Steven reached the foot of the grand staircase. He was sitting on one of the remaining grand chairs with his earphones in his ears. He pulled them out as Steven approached, grinned and touched his nose. They had history, Janek and Mr C.

''Lo, Mr C. Doing all right?'

'Just fine, Janek. And yourself?'

Janek looked the part, all right. Big and burly and good

in a uniform, he looked as if he could wrestle with a lion, but he had problems, many of them, including a predilection for tranquillisers and smokes on cold nights as well as warm ones, an undisclosed illness that lurked round his eyes and a fear of the dark. Janek should have been a custodian of a shop full of light and people rather than someone whose task it was to patrol an empty place with cavernous basements after dark. Janek liked clothes. It was not burglars he feared: he could cope with those, and who would want anything in here, anyway? No, it was the ghosts he feared, and he feared them mortally. Squatters was what the freeholders of the old bank feared, particularly those of the anti-capitalistic kind who would see adverse possession as a good joke. Janek was there to report squatters should they arrive, and then alert not the police but the owners, who would send a man along to pay them to go away.

Mr C had found him on night patrol once, soon after Mr C moved in. So many pills consumed, he had fallen asleep with the keys in his hand.

'Don't tell on me, please, Mr C. I need this job.'

'We need each other, Janek,' Steven had said. 'Come on, show me the basements.'

And Janek had. These days, he left the keys inside the

basement door, rather than carry them round. And by tacit arrangement, Steven could store what he liked down there, in the almighty safes if need be. All it took was praising Janek to his employers and the occasional twenty-pound note. They were allies, at least, not always pleased to see one another.

Exiting through the ridiculously grand doors, Steven smiled to himself. He supposed that the man in the portrait would have summoned his chauffeur, who would have doffed his cap. As it was, Steven Cockerel left the building without anyone noticing, looking just like anyone else. It was worth it. Old schoolchum Edward who he was due to see later, would be sick as a parrot.

He was going to earn the next million with his eyes and his fingertips and he was master of this small palace. Seagulls soared above the building, and he thought briefly of the sea.

Janek watched him go. He would leave the basement patrol until tomorrow. As long as Mr C was in residence, nothing wrong was going to happen.

'OK,' Sarah Fortune said to Di Porteous. 'Think of shopping as an adventure. Think of it as going to a gallery of paintings, looking at stuff. Waiting for the zing factor.'

'I hate shopping for clothes,' Di said. 'Thomas loved it.'

'Because it's like looking at paintings, looking at someone else's invention, looking at art on the hoof? Only the material's a bit different. You're still looking at inventions.'

'Problem is, you're looking at something to put on your back and carry round with you. Not the same as looking at paintings. You can't wear a painting.'

'Yes, you can,' Sarah said. 'Only if you're going to wear it every day, it'd better be beautiful and it'd better be good. Unlike a painting, you've got to be able to knock it about.'

'Get it dirty,' Di said.

'Dead right. And forget about what Thomas thought you ought to wear. Men are useless at this stuff. They think clothes are meant to impress.'

'Are they?'

'Define, rather than impress. As well as covering you up and keeping you warm. They're meant to give you a second skin. Preferably, one that goes with the skin you've got.'

I like being bossed about, Di thought to herself, as long as it's the same thing as learning something. Clothes as art? Well, well. Regard this whole enterprise as a learning curve. Thomas had been crap with clothes: as much as she had loved him, she did not always like his choices for either of them. Can't be good at everything.

A second skin? She liked that idea; a second, detachable skin to correspond with the first.

But clothes themselves, amassed in serried ranks in large shops, were another matter. It was as if she was looking at the forces of the enemy, sent to defy her, like looking at a whole load of disembodied things, hanging on hangers, limp and lifeless until touched and smelled.

'Always remember,' Sarah said, looking towards this hidden army, 'they need you more than you need them. They need us to bring them alive.'

It was still early for shoppers when they hit the first floor of the first shop in Oxford Street and all those clothes, just hanging around.

'First base,' Sarah said. 'Just feel stuff. Get to see how it feels. You must learn to feel if it's cotton, wool, silk. If it's none of those, you don't want it.'

She felt as if she were a mother leading a child.

'Colour?' Di asked.

'You know about colour, Di. Go for it. The best colours work best on cotton, wool, silk. Think about it. Think about how natural fabrics hold a pigment much better than plastic. It's acrylic versus oil. The better the fabric, the better the colour.'

Di looked. On a vast fashion floor, she went round like a sniffer dog. The brightest jewels of colour drew her first, along with the most muted. There were false lures, and she found them. An emerald green which proved to be false, a better green found only in cashmere, a dull green in a garment like grass which she touched and smelled as if she was about to eat it long before she looked at the shape of the thing. She passed on, eagerly at first, gradually getting slower. The shop filled and she became indifferent to the crowds.

'You keep going for green,' Sarah said.

'Thomas liked me in red.'

She was wearing a red T-shirt, for courage.

'Which has nothing to do with anything, if you don't mind me saying so. Red makes you shrink inside it. You've got to have something you want to put on first thing in the morning. Not something you shy away from but something you look forward to, so when you wake up in the morning you think, I want to wear *that*.'

'Brown,' Di said. 'Sand coloured.'

'No,' Sarah said firmly.

They continued. Sarah understood shape, Di went for colour. Gradually, Sarah corralled a number of garments over her arm, careful to choose with the other person in mind. Diana wanted something in which to hide: she had a sweet figure, requiring draping for emphasis, rather than hugging. Granta would have had her in shiny satin and false eyelashes, Sarah thought, irrelevantly. Granta misunderstood glamour. Glamour was something else. In the changing room, with Sarah looking on, Di scrambled into skirts and short, loose tops which skimmed her waist. No bows and the minimum of buttons. The effort of dressing and undressing made her more breathless than running on the beach. She acted up and pulled faces in the mirror, muttering to herself, Oh hell, until something, the least likely of all, seemed to transform her. Soft, full trousers, held at the ankles, and a linen top of soft green. Her brown skin shone in these, her eyes sparkled. She was suddenly made of bright but subtle colours, shapely in garments that made her stand straight, but in which she could also flop and run away.

'Don't change back,' Sarah said. 'Wear them now. Then we know what to look for.'

On the way out of the shop, Di stuffed the red T-shirt into a bin. Sarah watched, with quiet satisfaction. Di was getting the hang of this. Caffeine was needed.

'Where next?' Di said.

'Well, once we've established what sort of clothes might suit,' Sarah said, 'we home in on the kind of shops which have more of that kind of stuff and less of all the stuff we don't like. We've seen the broad canvas, now we go for the detail.'

'Sarah, why do people go for designer clothes?'

Di had cappuccino froth on her upper lip and her cheeks were flushed pink. Here was a woman who could take colour.

'Because they want to be designed? Because they want a label of authenticity? Because they can be a guarantee of beauty and style? Sometimes, not always. Because they show membership of a club? Also, there are such things as the emperor's clothes.'

'I know that story,' Di said, excited by the memory. 'The emperor's convinced by a whole lot of fraudsters that there is this marvellous, very expensive cloth of gold material which will make him look wonderful. Only snag is, it's so fine and refined, only highly intelligent people can see it and appreciate the quality. He can't see it, but he can't admit to *not* seeing it. So they wrap him round with the finest quality, magic garments and send him out to parade to his public. And everyone else has bought into the same story, so they can't admit the man is wearing nothing, so they ooh and ah, and ah and ooh and ahhh, because to do otherwise would make them stupid. Until some child pipes up and says, the emperor's naked.'

She wiped the froth from her lip with her sleeve and got up, ready to go.

'The thing is,' Sarah said, 'if the emperor had a sense of humour bigger than his vanity, he could have laughed it off, and said, hey, this is a joke, this is me without my second skin.'

'OK,' Di said. 'I want to see some emperor's clothes.'

'You already have,' Sarah said. 'They're everywhere. And if you can sort out the emperor's clothes in one area, like you do with your eyes for a painting, you can sort them out in another. You can be that child, who makes the obvious judgement, and says, this isn't real, this isn't good enough. That's what you do with a painting, isn't it?'

'I don't do anything of the kind,' Di protested. 'When I look at a painting, I want to like it. I want to like it so much it makes my heart sing.'

'That's what I'm like with clothes,' Sarah said. 'And men. Don't pick bad quality and anything you won't like the look of the next morning.'

'So nothing too funky, then,' Di said, grinning.

'I hate that word,' Sarah said, looking for a moment just

like her fastidious brother. 'Especially when applied to clothes.'

She braced her shoulders, sat up straight, ran her fingers through her hair so that her red curls stood to attention. She looked determined and zealous, her smile as wide as the sky. Di thought she was as beautiful as any painting.

'Come on,' Sarah said. 'We've only just started.'

'Remember what you promised?'

'Oh? What was that?'

'You said we'd look at paintings, too.'

'Yes, so we are. We're going to look at clothes inside paintings.'

It was two hours later that they reached the National Portrait Gallery, which had always seemed, to Sarah's eye, to be devoted to clothes. A lover of costume always looked for that first, and this gallery was a feast. People painted in their best: persons of fame not always painted entirely as they wished to be seen, perhaps, revealing more of themselves than they may have liked, but always dressed. Persons of distinction in whatever century, even the artists themselves, were rarely painted nude. None of these subjects would have fallen for the emperor's invisible cloth of gold: they would have chosen their apparel for the occasion of the portrait with great care. It would be tactile, it would be real; it would be bedecked with jewels for the Tudors, languid and loose for the poets of the twentieth century. It would be wafting silk or scarlet chiffon and corsets for those from the stage, dishevelled, crushed linen for the clubbable roué, a stern lack of care for the scientist, and all the while, each made a statement through their clothes, let alone their faces, their eyes, their hair. So much of their sense of self was expressed through what they wore, these people mostly dead, brought vividly alive.

For a person devoted to clothes, Sarah always looked at them first. Here you had a potted version of fashion from the Tudors to the twenty-first century. That's why she liked this place: art was fine, yes, she had a brother devoted to it, but she herself was there for the finery. As far as the artist was concerned, he was only as good as the clothes he painted. Seriously frivolous, Saul said. I rejoice in it, Sarah said.

'OK, Sarah, I see what you mean, clothes are important, OK?' Di said, transfixed by a picture of a Tudor lady, the wife of a nobleman with a waist as narrow as the span of her hand, the portrait of her elongated for elegance, with the jewels on her bodice and in her hair transfixing the eye of the beholder as much as the exquisite lace of her ruff, the details of which contrasted with the glorious paleness of her skin and her steadily vacant eyes.

'Not your style,' Sarah whispered to Di. 'They were sewn into their underwear for winter, those days.' By now, they were facing a portrait of the red-haired Queen Elizabeth the first, impossibly bedecked with the prettiest emblems of power, from roses to pearls, to uncut diamonds and gold lace. 'Remember someone said of her, "Queen Elizabeth taketh a bath once a month, whether she need it or no."'

'Lovely smell. Head lice. The pox.'

In the crowded and reverential galleries of the Tudors, surrounded by puzzled and bored schoolchildren looking for escape, it was easy to giggle, with giggles growing into the kind of uncontrollable snorting noises that carried them upstairs and then down again and out into the air, still faintly helpless. Like laughing in church, a heady gratitude to be living where they did, when they did, and not be a person of distinction who was sewn into clothes and never had a shower.

'What do people do now, to show off?' Di asked. 'Look dirty? Wear as little as possible?'

'That's about it,' Sarah said. 'Going naked got the emperor noticed. Can we do a detour?'

They were laden with noisy bags as they moved into the quiet environs of Jermyn Street. Men's clothes of a certain kind predominated in these shop windows and the

Arcade; shirts of severe stripes for the suited, shoes for the respectably booted, a place devoted to embroidered waist-coats, the back of Fortnum and Mason. Burberry, shirts, shoes, tweeds, for the young and elderly fogey. A small-scale street between big, important thoroughfares full of important businesses such as wine merchants, leading on to a parade of fine Victorian, huge-scale buildings. Coming out of low-lying Jermyn Street, walking to the east end of it, and seeing the huge thoroughfare beyond, was like going into a canyon of sound so great, the buildings were irrelevant until she looked. Sarah guided Di to the other side of the road across two sets of traffic lights and pointed at a building on the corner of the quiet street and the greater one. The building was a Victorian institution, heavily embellished, with grand front doors as tall as a passing bus, and inside she could imagine the grandest of entrance halls. And yet, it looked empty. Big windows on the raised ground floor, less big on the second, although still big and monumental, progressively smaller on the third, fourth and the fifth attic floor. A pitched roof above.

'Used to be a bank,' Sarah yelled over the sound of three lanes of traffic. They had retreated to the far side of the road. Sun glinted on the many windows of the corner building, glinted and darted, the interior forever invisible.

'Looks like it,' Di said. 'Safer than houses.'

The sun retreated behind cloud, deadening the glare and the noise. Di was clutching shopping bags and feeling insanely cheerful. As the light softened, she concentrated on the contours of the building as if she was looking at a painting or, by now, a dress. It was a well-dressed building, still wearing its original clothes of ornate plasterwork and carved wood and pristine grandeur. Sarah pointed to the third floor up, the floor below the small windows in the attic roof.

'Could you smash that window with a stone?' she yelled, over the sound of a revving bus. 'That one, there?'

'What?'

'Could you break that window, that one there?'

She was pointing, stabbing above her head, trying to be precise.

'Oh yes, for sure,' Di said. 'Easy.'

'Oh good,' Sarah said. 'That's where Granta's son lives.'

Di looked at the façade, with its heavy-lidded windows and the protruding sills and all that embellishment; no smooth, modern finish here. She could see herself climbing up the front from floor to floor.

'It looks like a bank. It is a bank. He lives in a bank?' she said, incredulously.

'Bless,' Sarah said. 'He does. Where else should a rich young man live, except in a converted bank, with money in the walls?'

Di looked up at the building again, memorising it. She noticed seagulls, wheeling above, a reminder of the river and the sea.

'Did you mean to bring us this route?' she said.

'Of course I did,' Sarah said. 'I hate wasting time. But it's maybe time to go home.'

'Time to go home,' Di echoed. 'First, we've got to buy presents. Something for Peg and something for Jones. And a hat for Saul. Did you know, he imagines his thought processes are improved by wearing a hat?'

'Haven't you noticed,' Sarah said, 'that Saul likes to dress like a late nineteenth-century Impressionist artist? Always a hat, especially in summer?'

'So he does,' Di said, fingering the stone in her pocket. 'Would you like me to smash the window now?'

She drew a smooth, grey stone out of her handbag and raised her arm.

'Stop!' Sarah said.

Di smiled and put the stone back.

A thief, living in a bank. Yes.

CHAPTER SIX

Late evening and still light.

Saul, wearing a straw hat tipped to the back of his head, tapped on the keys of his laptop, spoke on the phone, gathering information from a network of contacts who were not the same as friends, but useful gossipers all the same. Saul was light in his friendships; as long as he was discreet and amusing, he received information. Otherwise he found it by more direct routes, like breaking and entering, as he had with Thomas's children, while Thomas was alive. Particularly son-in-law Edward. They should be spent forces, those children, but Saul knew better than to ignore a bomb just because it was partially defused. Memory was short while malice always had a longer life.

He became increasingly irritable, not only because the two women in his life were both absent and together, but also because he was discovering more about this Steven Cockerel than he liked. And then Edward's name turned up, like a footnote on a page. Another, sinister complication. Concentrate on Steven.

It would seem, from what he could gather, that Steven Cockerel was on a crusade, or at least an experiment. Saul was in an unusually introspective mood and the pink of the evening sky encouraged it. He was musing on the nature of collectors and their strange, sometimes benign greed. He paced the room, looked out and down at the beach which did not transfix him. He could see himself lounging on it in a suit or a smock, accompanied by Sarah as his muse, wearing a bonnet and carrying a parasol. He was thinking of a painting, of course, seeing himself in it. Manet on a beach with his wife, Suzanne, painted in 1873; the man more enigmatic than the woman, his face hidden by his hat, the dark clothes stark against the sand and the creamy foam of the water beyond. Everything Saul saw became translated into a painting. He blinked and the deserted seashore was boringly bland. He took off the hat. Where was he? Ah, yes – collectors, envy, that kind of thing.

The more he discovered by rumour, the more he envied Mr Cockerel, and the more he worried. Envy was the wrong word to apply to a rich, wannabe collector. Saul no longer envied those with the money to collect tastefully and joyfully as Thomas had, although such envy had afflicted him in youth. His own attitudes had progressed beyond a desire for ownership or money. He preferred to be the agent and the hunter rather than the owner: it was enough for him to amass beautiful work, preserve it, live among it. You know, he said to the sky and the beach, yet again seeing himself upon it in an elegant pose, that playing the violin in this game is better than being the conductor. Getting things into the right, respectful hands, was it. Steven Cockerel was not the right pair of hands.

He lit a cigarette and coughed, mightily. Such a poisonous pleasure.

This man would not be the first of his type to find such an outlet for his nouveaux riches. Collecting was a disease afflicting oligarchs, tycoons of all nationalities, royalty, courtiers, merchants, pop stars and ordinary folk with twopence to rub together, gamblers, travellers, officers and other ranks. Only the motive was different. For the aristocratic English collectors of other centuries, it was an obsession with other cultures and the desire to bring them home. They swooped upon Venice, Florence, Amsterdam and exported the very artists to put them to work in their own back yards. A thirst for decoration? A search for identity? Status? Hardly the motive of the marauding general in times of war, taking whatever he could get to feather his nest. Those sort of collectors were only pirates. Steven Cockerel fell into that category. Saul tried to be as charitable as Di might have been, but then Di was perversely charitable. The motives of most collectors were mixed.

Not quite the case, here. Steven was simply trying to acquire *things* which he might be able to sell at a great profit in the future. Buy cheap, sell dear. What was more, he appeared to have studied the other capitalists who had got their fingers burned in the money-laundering art world, and he was not going to burn his own in the same way. No video installations, no dead sheep, no utterly perishable crap that was going to rot, no sensationalism. No talked-up stuff and nonsense spoken of in hushed, humourless tones as worth a future fortune. No, Steven concentrated on items of painting and sculpture made of fabric that would last for ever. He may as well have been investing in a mine. Dig it out, buy it, hide it away: sell to highest bidder.

Nothing wrong with that, Saul supposed. He could scarcely afford the moral high ground himself, having been perfectly capable of cheating and lying and, once, as Edward knew, rather good at it. It was the approach that Steven seemed to have adopted to the whole thing that he disliked.

Buy cheap. Which meant, so rumour had it, and there was never smoke without fire in that small world, that Steven Cockerel swooped on the impoverished owner desperate to sell and beat them down even further than they were willing to go. Thomas had never done that, but Saul had, before he met Thomas. *Quality is never cheap,* Thomas said. *You can steal from fools who have no respect or knowledge for what they have, but never force anyone to part with what they love.*

Right now, Saul had the recognition of one opportunist for another and a strange feeling of being copied on his way to becoming a grown-up. He stepped back to the view of the beach, seeking perspective. At the same time, a rancorous posse of gulls on evening exercise crowded against the great windows of the great room, and he stopped to wonder at them. A crowd of scavengers, excited by a promise of food, shrilling with the apprehension of denial and filling the sky in a great, noisy chorus. Di loved them and fed them. Saul slightly feared them; he preferred the urban variety and longed for his London streets. He told himself that he loved nothing but paint and canvas, in comparison to which his love for a very few human individuals was a relatively small, if inconveniently persistent heartbeat.

Roll on, Steven Cockerel, with your ugly name. Miserable capitalist. I do not like you, and I do not like the fact that you went to the same school as Edward, the thieving son-in-law of my patron, Thomas.

The one thing he could not find was an image of the man. A very private individual who lived above a bank, and whatever he looked like, he was hiding that, too.

Peg came in, accompanied by a vacuum cleaner. Her lustrous hair, currently black, was piled on top of her head. She wore huge, hooped earrings and her lips were scarlet. She was towing the hoover like a well-tamed pet on a lead. There was an extravagant feather duster over her shoulder and she was a woman on a mission. A woman, now, not the girl she had been the year before and not the androgynous kind Saul preferred, like Di, who was a whole lot less threatening. Peg looked him in the eye, reminding him that on his short list of people he liked and almost loved, Peg was not included, although faintly admired and held in something like affection for her devotion to cleanliness. He loathed the sound of a vacuum cleaner.

'Must you?' he said. 'At this time of evening?'

'Yes, I must, dumbo. Thursdays I work all day, don't I?'

Peg worked four days as a trainee at the local hairdresser. He remembered.

'She'll be coming back sooner or later. I've got a job to do, and Di likes clean, so do you, so put up and shut up and get outta this room for an hour. Besides, I want to talk to you.'

Saul turned off his laptop with obvious fastidiousness. 'Well, talk, why don't you?'

She was right, of course: dust settled in this dead man's rooms daily, wind penetrated through windows, bringing more. The house depended a lot upon Peg for its wholesome qualities, but his liking of her well-paid, zealous services was not without suspicion. The feeling was mutual. She turned on the vacuum cleaner and started work, pushing the nozzle against the carpet like someone attacking an overgrown lawn.

'What did you want to talk about?'

He was yelling over the noise before it stopped and he found himself yelling anyway. She always got him on the wrong foot.

She looked at him as if he was mad or invisible; he wasn't sure which.

'Them bones in the cellar,' she shouted, turning on the hoover again. 'Bloody mess, they are.'

'What?'

She shrugged and hoovered, earrings jangling.

'I told you. You heard.'

He left the room. He had not really heard, wouldn't believe her if he had.

Fine. Peg paused. She would dust every picture with this fine, huge, ostrich feather duster she had; a work of art, that, pretty with it. Every ounce of pesky dust to be got up out of the floor and walls and into the mouth of this hoover, and don't bloody disturb me. And, if you don't listen to me about bones you never told me about and think I never knew about, well don't. See if I care, I've said it.

The house was empty without Di in it, even when Jones was there, which he wasn't all the time. It was at its very best when everyone was there, with Patrick and fights about bedtime. Peg wasn't going to leave, not yet. Didn't matter that Saul didn't notice her; he didn't hate her or anything, just didn't notice, fine. Jones not noticing her was another matter. Every other bloody fucker thinking she was deaf and blind was something else entirely.

Long after she'd finished and gone down to the kitchen, leaving Saul in possession of a clean room, there was a clamour at the back door and Di was back with bags of shopping. It seemed that Sarah woman was a good influence. Way to go, Di. Good girl. Time you got new clothes, and now I can have all of your old ones. And then there was the booming voice of Jones who had met Di at the station, saying what the fuck? Presents for everyone, half the shopping was presents for everyone else. Silly Di. You know what? Peg said to herself. I love you to bits, Di, but not as much as I love Jones, even though he doesn't listen to me either.

These are amazing shoes, Di. You always get the shoes right, cos we're the same size.

I might wear them tomorrow, when I go out to work. I'm going to see if I can find your dad. I know where he's hiding. Monica, my other boss, she more or less told me. Monica'll like these shoes.

Peg left them all chatting away and went upstairs. There were too many times when she just didn't belong with the grown-ups. She needed more than this and she was going to get it, and at the same time she felt absurdly responsible for them. They had sorted out her life, and she was going to sort out theirs. Besides, hadn't Di taught her the way? Hadn't she said as much? Always try and befriend the enemy. It's the only way to find out how much you risk before you throw a stone at them.

Two miles away, Sarah got home. The contrast to London always delighted her. She lived in a small terraced cottage in Warbling, rented from Granta, who lived next door and owned three houses. Sarah had achieved an ambition to own nothing and thought gratefully of the complications that avoided. She could not go on like this for ever, but it was OK for now.

There were messages from Granta on her landline; there had been three text messages from Granta during the day. Sarah went round as darkness fell.

'How did it go?' Granta said as she opened the door. 'Is she hooked?'

Sarah sat on a stool in an overcrowded room, which bore all the evidence of someone who had moved in from a much larger place. It was a foil to her own minimalism, but oddly comfortable.

'Hooked on clothes? Not quite. It'll take more than that. I don't like the word "hooked".'

'So many words you don't like. Don't you like the word "hooked" because you're a hooker?'

'My, my, Granta, dear, you are scratchy this evening. I was never a hooker. I was a peacemaker, who could use the medium of sex to smooth troubled waters. Not the same thing.'

Granta was almost remorseful, but not quite. Anxiety always made her bitchy and aggressive. The house was overfull, the walls full of pictures, good and bad, albeit with notable gaps on the walls.

'I'm sorry,' she said. 'I'm envious. Diana Porteous has got her life ahead of her, and I haven't. And I would like to be going shopping with a figure like that.'

Sarah sighed.

'I've warned you about envy, haven't I? It's awful, horrible stuff like black tar that gets into your lungs. You don't really want the pictures back, do you?'

She gestured towards the spaces on the walls, earmarked with ghostly, dusty outlines from where they had hung for at least two years in this room with a fire. Quite small pictures, she guessed from the shadows they left.

'No, of course I don't want them back, I've said so. If I get them back, I'll give them away to a proper collection. I'll give them to Saul.'

'So,' Sarah said evenly, 'you don't really care about the pictures he took. But you might care about Steven. What you want is Steven. You want to bring Steven back.'

'My bloody husband wouldn't let me have children,' Granta yelled. 'He wouldn't give me the chance of other babies, so that I could look after Steven. He might as well have been my own flesh and blood.'

'But he wasn't. He isn't. He was his father's bastard child.'

'And I loved him to bits,' Granta said. 'And when he was small, he loved me.'

'Children leave, Granta. Even your own flesh and blood leave. That's what they're supposed to do. You don't own them.'

'Everybody leaves me,' Granta yelled. 'I never get anything I want.'

'You've got a room with a view,' Sarah said. 'Look at the moon and have a gin. You're solvent, and you're gorgeous even when you're ghastly.'

Granta sniggered.

'What a manipulative female you are, Sarah.'

'Takes one to know one,' Sarah said cheerfully and went for the drinks.

Granta liked a drink and hated to drink alone. At what

point it was that *in vino veritas* kicked in, Sarah was still unsure. Granta usually told it as it was, but not always. Sarah brought out Granta's present from London, which was cheese from Paxton and Whitfield in Jermyn Street, and wafer-thin biscuits from Fortnum and Mason on the corner. Granta laughed. It was her saving grace that, spiteful and self-pitying though she might be, marooned as she might be, she could laugh at her own tantrums and apologise.

'I'm wrong,' she said, sipping and savouring. 'I do sometimes get what I want. Like now, only I just don't get it often enough. Steven was always passionate about cheese.'

Something occurred to Sarah, which made her shift uneasily.

'Did he live here as a boy? When you were in the big house at the top of the hill? Or were you still in London?'

Granta waved her free hand airily, looking shifty.

'Oh yes, some of the time. Before he went away to school.'

Sarah sat upright. Always wise to be alert when Granta was shifty and she was aware that it was easier to be fond of this awkward old cow more times than others.

'So did he know Thomas's children? Not far away.'

'I suppose so.' Just as airily spoken. 'Similar ages, all that.'

103

'And he would have been to Thomas's house?'

'For sure, when he was little, but he wasn't interested in paintings then. What child is?'

He is now, Sarah thought and didn't say so. Continued on a conversational note.

'So, I suppose he knows about the current state of affairs, then, Di being widowed and all that?'

Granta's patience snapped, despite the cheese. She knew when she was being cross-examined.

'Not from me, he doesn't. He doesn't communicate with *me*. But he did go to school with Edward who married one of the awful daughters. Old chums, maybe.'

Her eyes misted. The critical point of *in vino veritas* had come and gone.

'So what does he look like, your Steven?' Sarah asked. 'Have you got a photo?'

'I tore them up, I told you, but oh, he was a beautiful boy. Quite gorgeous. Blond hair and blue, blue eyes. I always knew he was going to be tall. My husband had him booked for the playing fields of Winchester. Odd, when he came from Huddersfield. But then again, his mother was pretty. Even though I say stepson, I mean adopted son. My husband fucked the cleaning lady and picked up the result.'

Sarah took a deep breath. Too much gin. She offered more of the cheese. Thought of Granta Cockerel alone in London. *In vino veritas* might be fantasy, and she would have to find out.

'Hello, old chum.'

'Halloah, Ted.'

Edward hated being called Ted.

'How's life, then, Stevie boy?'

Steven Cockerel hated being called Stevie.

'Not so hot,' Edward said. 'I'm not talking to my wife and my son hates me and I've got flu, but otherwise everything's fine, ha ha. What'll you have?'

'Becks,' Steven said. 'Don't worry, I'll get it.' Thinking at the same time how Edward failed the first test in any negotiation. Never admit to illness or failure, never invite pity, always recite your last success.

They were in a dark, unreconstructed pub in St James's that was still hung about with the gloom of ages. There were yellowed prints and a murky patina on the walls that made Steven shudder. He had known that Edward would wait for him to buy the first round and would probably expect him to buy the second, and if Steven suggested dinner, he would buy that, too.

'About these paintings,' he said. He wasn't going to waste time on reminiscence or family detail.

'The Fragonard and the Gainsborough,' Edward said. His eyes were bloodshot.

'The paintings your wife's father gave to you, you say. Which you now want to sell. The ones you showed me in your delightful home.'

'The very same, old chum.'

'Ten thousand the pair,' Steven said, flatly.

The bloodshot eyes burned bright with anger.

'You little shit, Stevie. You joke. You know they're worth much more than that. Minimum of a hundred thousand, possibly more than that.'

Steven shrugged. 'Not to me, they aren't.'

Edward looked at him with loathing. Steven, old chum, two years younger, but on the same teams at school, who had turned out to be everything he wanted to be, namely rich and ruthless. Old acquaintance kept the loathing under wraps, along with the observation that Stevie was a whole foot shorter.

'But the fact of the matter is, old chum,' Steven continued, 'they aren't the genuine articles. The Gainsborough is not painted by Gainsborough but by his nephew and only pupil, Dupont. Who learned to paint exactly in the style of his uncle, perhaps with greater freedom. Remained modest and unknown. And the famous Fragonard, the girl on the swing, wasn't painted by Jean-Honoré, but by Marguerite Gérard, his pupil and sister-in-law who lived with him and his wife. Oh yes, they're beauties in their own right, and yes, worth a lot. But not yet and not now, because you put them up for auction last year, and they were withdrawn at the last minute. Someone found out. Now, as everyone knows, once they've been withdrawn from sale like that, they lose all credibility for a long while, and you can't put them back on the market for a year or two. Time has to pass. And they'll always be a little bit tainted and it'll always be known they were withdrawn once. So how about a bird in the hand?'

'Not that kind of bird,' Edward said.

He could feel tears pricking his eyelids, swallowed hard. Steven could almost have felt sorry for him if he had that kind of sentiment in him.

'That bitch,' Edward said. 'That absolute bitch. She palmed us off with the second best. That bitch.'

'They aren't second best,' Steven said. 'They're fantastic but they aren't named commodities. Which bitch is this?'

'My father-in-law's wife,' Edward said, clenching his

fist to stop his hand trembling. 'Diana Porteous. Wife of Thomas Porteous.'

Memory came upon Steven like a great, crashing tidal wave. Memory of a house by the sea and being taken for tea. The memory engulfed him, paralysed him for a minute.

The bar was emptying.

'She made sure we got second best,' Edward said. Then he looked at Steven shrewdly.

'What if I were to tell you how to lay your hands on something better? Something very pretty and vulnerable. And then maybe you might consider offering me a lot more.'

'I'm all ears,' Steven said.

He pushed his hair out of his eyes and fetched another brandy.

You've opened a real can of worms, old chum.

CHAPTER SEVEN

Picture. *Woman in evening dress, kissing her children goodbye before going out for the evening.*

It took half a day for the retail therapy of London to work a certain kind of magic, and by the afternoon, concentration restored, Di was fit to get down to serious work. It was the clothes that did it, made her focus in a way she had not for months; she was recognising the other importance of clothes.

In the year before Thomas's death, she had catalogued the whole Porteous collection, with slightly quixotic notes on every painting and drawing, with half of the factual detail on the many anonymous works coming from educated guesswork. She needed to refine it. She had lost heart for the task, but the clothes inspired her to begin again. The paintings, in the main, were painted between 1850 and 1960. She could estimate the approximate decade in which a painting had been done, or at least the era, by the paint, the prevailing styles and themes, sometimes the framer's notes on the back and other extraneous details. Now she was dating them by garments, thinking the whole thing through with a fresher mind.

Nothing dated a painting with figures more accurately than the clothes they were wearing. Fashion trends rarely lasted more than a decade, although they could come back, years later, but never quite the same or in the same material. She could define the age of a painting by the type of pigment, because the artist could only use what was available and affordable at the time: it could be a guide to forgeries, but she was not looking for that. She was looking to give closer-than-approximate dates to undated things, the better to organise the whole collection. A room for each decade, perhaps, enough to give it an historical perspective so that you could travel through it in time. Organised that way, she would be able to see the gaps that existed to be filled. Thomas had wanted to represent all the forgotten artists of his own century, with the rough theme *Pictures that people would really like to see and can't,* but for all that, Thomas, and latterly Di, had gone with their eyes and bought, randomly. Never mind the theme; if the painting inspired and delighted, and had real integrity, they would go for it whatever the subject and whatever the decade of origin, even if there were already something similar on the wall. Nor were the pictures hung in any thematic way; they were displayed in accordance with favouritism and their various needs for light. But there must be a theme, Saul had argued, so that it flows and the outsider can follow it all and see where it goes. And then we know where it should go next. Then we fill in the gaps, because all collections must change and grow to stay alive.

There were other ways to organise a collection, Di decided, and stopped looking with such fascination at the clothes. She could organise it purely by subject matter. There could a room full of men, a room full of children, another of landscape and seascape. Then she wondered, alarmed by the notion, would the women in the paintings in *that* room get bored with looking at one another? Would the men in *their* quarters start to scowl and become competitive with their all-male company and want to join the women? How could she separate Madame de Belleroche from her flirting courtier at the far end of the room? Di talked to pictures: she knew they were alive and she was sentimental enough to want the subjects in the paintings to have their own, interesting view. So, putting together all the paintings that featured children – of which there were many – would be a bit like leaving a school classroom unsupervised. God alone knows what they would get up to when everyone else was in bed.

She laughed at herself.

No. Leave it random. Let children on a beach sit alongside a bowl of winter flowers. But, if the collection was mirroring its own day and age, it needed more of the brickwork, more of the urban, perhaps.

By evening, she was thoroughly confused, but she knew she had worked well, leaving her mind scrambled with images, the way she liked it. All those clothes. She visualised a picture of a shop floor, like Selfridges.

Then Patrick phoned, as he often did without ever confessing to his mother, needing a bulletin on what was happening with the sea. She could picture him on the line, with his specs crooked. 'I've been drawing a lot and keeping a diary,' he whispered. 'You know I'm only let out on licence, so I've been very good and quiet and Mum says I can come to you at the weekend cos they want to go somewhere.'

'Somewhere nice, I hope,' Di said politely.

'Don't know. Something funny's going on here,' Patrick whispered. 'Daddy's got an old chum who's been round looking at the pictures Grandpa gave them. They talked about you, too. Mummy doesn't like him. I drew him when he wasn't looking. Dad pinched some of my drawings to show him. Can I come?'

'Yes,' Di said. 'Yes! Yes, yes!'

'Have they finished all the digging on the beach?'

'Yup, so there's nothing to look at all.'

'You're joking,' he said fervently.

Talking about you to an old chum. Di did not like that. She had a sudden image of that bank building in Pall Mall and a desire to throw stones. Maybe it was a little anarchic anger at the place that had helped inspire a day's concentration. The call from Patrick saddened and delighted her, reminded her how duplicitous she had become. So much Patrick knew and so much he didn't. Di took her work downstairs. The legend handed down to Patrick was that his mother and father, Gayle and Edward, had simply collected the Gainsborough and the Fragonard, which were theirs. No mention to him that Gayle was caught on camera, beating the shit out of Di, while Edward was equally captured for posterity, wrecking the cellar in his search for treasure. Di disliked the necessary blackmail. The price they paid was to leave her alone and to allow Patrick to visit a place he loved. And the price I pay, Di thought, is never to tell the boy and make him unhappy. That silence should last for ever. There was a vivid memory of that night of hatred that nagged at her. A memory of her father coming into the room. She went back to pen and paper and found herself drawing a sketch of the bank where Steven Cockerel lived.

Poor, fitful sleep, featuring clothes and bones, made her rise with the light and go straight out, an alternative to sitting in the long room and writing, following Thomas's dictate to write something every day. Clears the mind, he said; forces stray thoughts to have substance, like rain clouds. It makes them shed their load and move on.

Days like this, it was better to walk and do the writing in her head while moving. Besides, she wanted to see what had happened to the town end of the beach, now all the works were finished. Patrick had reminded her and she wanted to be able to report what the great, grand diggers had left. She too had been transfixed by them. That end of the beach had been her childhood playground while the less populated end with the big houses was where she lived now. An untrustworthy memory of her father persisted; she had glimpsed him here, earlier in the summer.

She was a whole mile from home, noticing how much the landscape had changed, and she was walking on it as if it was new.

Much of the old, smooth shingle had been washed away over the years, leaving sand visible at low tide. Replenishing the shingle had raised the level of the beach by several metres. New shingle had been pumped ashore and distributed over the wealth of the old, so that the top covering of the beach now consisted of hundreds of tons of ballast, half sand, half mismatched, sharp-edged stone excavated from far away and dumped here. The new stone was alien; it did not react like the old stone, did not slip and slide and rearrange its own rounded surfaces into smooth slopes when shifted by the tide. Instead, the sandy ballast broke into brittle, steep ledges, the angry water dragging away the sand and leaving rough stones marooned on a ridge. The whole configuration of the north beach had changed, so that the area nearest the sea at low tide was pebbly sand, separated from the rest by a high, steep bank. Easier to walk by the very edge of the water at low tide, strolling along on a flat surface, with the ridge rendering all who walked there invisible from the road above, but there was danger in reaching it. In time, people and dogs would make paths, but not yet. It was all too fragile and too new. Di was mourning the fact that the new shingle was so ugly: there were no ancient stones with a hole all the way through, no variation in colour. None of this stuff was fit for throwing and skimming, but then, she always carried her own. She thought of Sarah's shocked face when she had produced the stone in London, glad she would see her soon, because already she was talking to Sarah in a way she could to no one else and Sarah promised adventure. They were right about that; she needed it.

Di looked at the horizon and thought, never mind about the beach. The sea would do what the sea would do, and the old stone would resurface soon enough. She was wearing her new clothes, wearing them in, challenging them to see how they would last, while making comparisons with the stones in her pocket and the stones at her feet.

Then she felt the ridge crumble behind as a huge dog leapt over the escarpment, showering her with sharp little pebbles, stinging her legs and driving her upright, shouting. The dog carried on over her head, forced on by its own velocity, stumbling in its own mini-avalanche, tumbling and turning. A rust-coloured dog, which righted itself and turned from where it had tumbled halfway down to the sea, frightened by her shouting and standing, legs braced, its own anger and fear mirroring her own, pausing ominously, staring back at her, disorientated, balancing uneasily on the new surface in a state of shock. Di felt the smooth, weighty stone in her hand and raised her arm. In the split second of taking aim, she looked at the dog again, changed her mind, and flung the stone far over the animal's head. The dog paused for a split second, and instead of coming towards her, gazed briefly at the flight of the stone and bounded away after it.

A clumsy moving creature; hearing the splash of the stone as it entered the sea, dithering on the edge of waves, barking in puzzlement, paddling up and down in search of what it had lost. Di squatted on her haunches, laughing at it, daft beast. The dog gave up the chase and gambolled back towards her, tongue hanging out, begging for someone to play. She found herself looking round for the driftwood which had once littered the beach, found nothing for a dog to retrieve or chew. This beach was so cleansed, it was repellent. The rusty dog had a bark like a mournful foghorn and all she could find to throw was a piece of shell too light for the task.

'I don't suppose you want to keep her, do you?' a voice asked.

The hound was off, snuffing round with its ears trailing on the ground.

'No,' she said, turning to see who it was. There was a small, agile man, with a camera round his neck, a rucksack and stick, slithering down the grove left in the mini cliff by his dog which already seemed bigger than him.

'Only she's a rescue,' the man said in a sad voice. 'Highly neurotic. Known as Grace. She was a fraction of this size when my friend got her. Grown a bit. Soft as butter.'

'I did notice,' Di said. 'She's reminded me of something.'

'Oh?'

'Nothing, only the town motto. Befriend the enemy before you try to kill it.'

The hound was nuzzling at her feet, licking her sandals. She looked to the sky and felt an uplift of joy, like an escaped prisoner. That was the clue to it all: befriend the enemy. That was the clue to Granta's thief, to everything, including responsibility. Embrace the demons, then they can't tie you down. Get on with it. The dog seemed to have found a bone.

'You don't really mean it, do you, about getting rid of her?' she said.

'She isn't really mine to get rid of. I'm sorry she scared you and I'm glad you didn't hit her with that stone.'

The dog dropped, belly down, panting.

'You could easily have stopped her in her tracks,' the man said, not accusing, merely making an admiring observation to which she chose not to respond, thinking instead what a great daft dog this would be to have around when Patrick came to stay. He could play with a dog like this. She was remembering a scene from one of the paintings, children and dogs on shimmering sand, all of them yelling and dirty.

'You didn't get that stone from this beach,' he said. 'Which is a shame. Still, it's better than it was for walking a dog.'

'You local?' she asked.

''Fraid not. I'm here to survey the works and I make maps. I'm doing a survey of what you've gained and lost by this flood-defence stuff. My knowledge is purely professional. I'm sorry for what's lost, like driftwood to throw for a dog, and all those lovely, different-coloured stones. Mind you, when I'm surveying, I let the dog do most of it. She's better at it than me.'

She liked the tone of his voice, and anyone who made maps had her vote. Di loved maps. There were few enough people who loved stones and flint the way she did, and Patrick did, and Thomas had.

'Better stones down the other end,' she said. 'And driftwood. Flood defences don't apply down there. The sea creeps up from underneath, not over the top. It's a longer, steeper beach so they left us alone.'

'Yes,' he said. 'You'll get flooded about once a decade, right?'

They were already walking in that direction and kept on walking, Di loving the sight of the dog. She had not really taken in the man's face, save to say it was quite unremarkable in comparison to the animal. The man was bareheaded and clean-shaven, wore glasses, was scarcely taller than her, unthreatening and oddly familiar, somehow. He made her think of Patrick. Something boyish and apologetic about him, and he cared about stones.

'What do people think of the new beach, then?' he asked. 'See, the original idea was to dredge up the old shingle from offshore, the stuff that had been dragged away. Dredge it up and bring it back, but it was just too complicated. There's so much stuff, so many wrecks, we couldn't find a well of shingle. So we bought in new.'

120

'Inshore wrecks? I thought they were all on the Goodwin Sands.'

Mrs Porteous the first, wishing to be buried there. Don't think of that now.

'Oh yes, there's a few inshore wrecks, and lots of detritus. Nets and bits and pieces, stuff that's been dumped by trawlers long since, a lot of fly-tipping. Now, if the sea had dragged away the shingle and put it all in one safe place, that would be another matter. See over there?'

He spoke like a lecturer in a dry, didactic voice. She followed the direction of his pointing finger. Thought of the word for a hand used as a signpost. A manicule, yes, that was the word. He had a nice, clean manicule.

'There's a wreck there, see? Makes the water shallower, so that it's choppier when you go over it in a boat. Wrecks like that, with all sorts of sticky-up bits, are well charted. No fisherman goes near them, because they'll snarl their nets. Makes it the best place to bury a body at sea. Weight it with concrete, drop it on a pile of existing wreckage and nothing will disturb it. I made a map of the inshore wrecks. The clear spaces in the Channel, and the only places where you can have official burials. Oh look, I love this pier. Soon we'll be back to the old stone. Sorry, I talk too much.'

It had seemed effortless to walk beneath the pier at low

tide on the sandy side. More beautiful by far from beneath than it was above, with its stumpy legs forming an archway which seemed to reach to infinity. Soundless down here. The flood-defence ballast had filled the hollow gaps where the pier met the land, so that there was no space to shelter, smoke pot, hunker down. She wondered where her father was. They walked beyond, where the beach changed into its steep, smoother slopes, the man talking and Di enchanted by his knowledge: she was always enchanted by anyone with knowledge. She filled her pockets with three stones perfect for throwing. There was no more sand. The dog led the way uphill, back to the path, and then they were level with her house.

'This is where I live,' she said. 'Would you like to come in? I'm afraid the front door doesn't work.'

'This?' he said. 'According to my map, it's a schoolhouse. Or was.'

'Yes,' said. 'Once.'

'Ah,' he said. 'Another time, perhaps. I've got another mile to go, but thank you. I'm Tom Ryan, by the way.'

'I'm Di.'

'Best-dressed girl on the beach,' he said, smiling for the first time. 'Apart from Grace, of course. Your colours suit the landscape.'

She found herself blushing furiously.

'See you round,' she said.

The dog had found a piece of driftwood and dropped it at Di's feet. She handed it to the man and didn't turn back, even when she heard the hound scamper away down the noisy old shingle in pursuit.

There was nobody home. A man with knowledge, she thought; perhaps they would be friends. She was thinking, as she had often thought before, that what she would have liked above all things was a brother. Not some passing love affair, not going wild, but a brother, like Saul had a sister. Someone she had always known.

Where were they all? Peg at the hairdresser, learning how. Saul up in London, with his other clients, or wherever he was when he was not here, which could be days at a time. Jones in his own home, or fishing on the pier, ready to appear sometime soon. She had no control over anyone's movements and didn't wish it. Each could come and go, stay or not stay, they were not captives. She went upstairs to look through the window, not exactly to see where Tom Ryan had gone on his search for stones.

He was out of sight and she did not know whom she had liked best, him or the dog.

She felt ready to go back to work. A day of it, before

Sarah came over. Work, at long last, being able to concentrate and thinking in straight lines. Thinking she would like a painting of chimneys. There was a noise downstairs as Jones came crashing in.

'I saw you from the pier,' he yelled. 'Walking along with a fella. What's that all about?'

'He's a surveyor, surveying the beach,' Di said, wearily. 'Met him down the other end.'

'Surveyor?'

'Surveyor and map maker. With a dog.'

Jones relaxed. Persons accompanied by dogs were OK. She hadn't let him in. He was suddenly ashamed of his vigilance, could see how it looked. As if he was always keeping an eye on her from his vantage point on the pier. It was true, he was. Stupid, really. There was nothing he could do about anything when she was out of sight.

'Sorry, Di, only he looked a bit fucking shifty. And he's short.'

In Jones's book, being on the short side was a crime. Small men packed a mean punch. They were overly ambitious and used knives rather than fists.

'OK, then,' he said. 'Fancy a bit of breakfast?'

'Great, if you're going to cook it. Then I'm going to work.'

'Well, glory be. About time. Got a good man coming in to talk about repairs next week, OK?'

He busied himself with finding the right pan, whistling to the eggs as he broke them into a bowl.

'And we've got Patrick for the weekend.'

'Great,' Jones said with slightly false enthusiasm. 'Better stock up, then. Boy eats like a horse. Peg'll be pleased. Very pleased, she loves that lad. Peg's doing ever so well, isn't she, Di?'

'Yes, she is.'

'They love her in the hairdresser's,' he rattled on. 'Monica says she's a natural. Works hard, good with the customers. Really likes to experiment, wants to learn. Brings in a younger clientele. Mon reckons she's going to be stylist to the stars. Anyway, she just seems so much more confident, Peg does. I'm proud of her.'

Peg, Jones's protégée, although it was Di who rescued her. He was right about Peg, though. She knew her own mind, developed her own authority.

'Born organiser. Mustn't ever treat her like a fool,' Di said.

'Me?' Jones said. 'As if I would.' He was a noisy cook, always talked better when cooking. 'Only there's one thing worrying me. About her.'

'Spit it out.'

Jones couldn't quite. Couldn't quite say, well you know Quig's around, I think he might use Peg to get to you. And Peg likes the older blokes, but no, that was daft. Instead he said, 'Well, she does go to some of the rougher pubs, you know.'

'Jones, she's a Londoner and she's seen the inside of a prison,' Di said, gently. 'I think she'll cope. Wouldn't put it past her if she was canvassing for new clients.'

He laughed out loud. 'Wouldn't she just?'

Jones loved Peg. It was a pity she was too young.

The smell of bacon was the best in the world.

Yeah, Peg knew her own mind. She could fix things for people and she wanted to do more of it. Later in the day, she was in the hairdresser, liking the fact that she was trusted so much that she was left to sweep up and lock up on half-day closing while Monica went out. Loved the run of the place, but she wasn't working, she was facing this old man who had wandered in, asking for Monica. Skulked in, more like, in the same way he'd skulked in a few times before over the last months and then shifted off. He always came at the wrong time, and as it turned out, Monica didn't want to see him any more, although she had told Peg who he was, as if she didn't know already. Mon always tried to get out of town on half-day closing.

Old bloke. Everyone over fifty was old in Peg's eyes, and the poor buggers always seemed to need sleep and couldn't hold their drink, from what she could see. Not that that made them any different from the young ones who were daft enough to shave off their hair. She knew who this old man was, of course she did. He was Di's dad, and his name was Quig, and he was supposed to be mad, bad, and dangerous to know, blah, blah blah. Bollocks. She'd seen him first when he'd hit Jones on the pier, all that time ago, and he could scarcely make a dent, even then. For heaven's sake, he was just old, shuffling in, and he had a fantastic pile of thick grey hair. Peg had wanted to talk to him for a while. Maybe she just had a penchant for old men, but there again, they did have better hair. So when this one stood, looking a bit tired, she said off the top of her head, 'You didn't pass on your hair to that daughter of yours, did you?' And he said, 'My daughter? What daughter?' and looked as if he was going to cry.

Sit down and get your hair washed at least, she said. Monica used to do that for him, or so she told Peg. He's got a fantastic head of hair, Monica said, only good thing about him. Anyway, he sat down by the basin as directed. Whether he knew he was going to get a soaking, she didn't know, he submitted anyway.

Peg had noticed how much people talked when they were being washed and blow-dried. It was one of the things she loved about the whole thing. What else could you do, when doing this, but make people feel happier? When she was working on one of those cruise ships she spied on the horizon through her iPhone, they would have better chairs than this but you bet your sweet life they'd still talk and she'd listen. In this line of business, you were always going to make the customer happier than when they came in, even when they grumbled. Unless you burned their scalps and she knew how not to do that, even though it was sometimes tempting.

A certain smell rose off Quig, not too bad, but something she noticed. A mixture of salt, sweat, tears, aftershave and animal. He was the one who hit Jones on the night she'd met Jones, after Di had paid her railfare and got her as far as the pier, and it was Jones who took her to Di's place. And this daft old man wanted Monica who didn't want him, although once upon a time she had hinted she did his hair for free, just like she used to for Jones, and Peg knew about wanting someone who didn't want you. Liked them both, Peg guessed, not that Monica said so. Nobody told her anything except by accident, as if she didn't have ears. Look at him. Dangerous? You're joking, Peg said to herself. Yes, she did want to talk to Quig. Seemed to her that Di was a bit hard on Quig.

When you washed someone's hair, they turned into dummies. There was a whiff of vodka on his breath. Not quite drunk, almost there; not quite filthy, but on the way. Mumbling and obedient. Like her dad. Lean back, she said, and he did. His hair was a joy, because there was lots of it, long, thick, curly and ripe for experiment. The man had pride, she noticed, however he lived he managed to shave every day, so his chin was clean. Better blow it dry, she was thinking. You don't put a man under a helmet-shaped dryer, they get restive. He was a good customer. Talked all the time. Give them a prompt and they usually did.

'You're Di's dad, aren't you? Where'd you get this lovely hair? Lovely hair you've got. Hers isn't like that.'

'She got hers from her mother.'

'Really?' she said, washing away. He was a strange, still man, and while thinking he was an old man and not being in the least afraid of him, she was wary. That smell, that negligence: here was another person who knew the inside of a prison. She could see it now, feel the grease and taste the awful food. Everyone bad-mouthed Quig. She knew what that felt like and she knew what it was like to be a leper and she knew it didn't mean you were sick all the way through, you could still have useful hands. So what if he was supposed to have done some crap things? So had she, and she was learning that didn't make her a bad person. Just made her a person who deserved a second chance, and maybe he did too. With hair like this he deserved it.

Her ministrations seemed to make him drowsy. He wasn't talking in sequence, but he was talking; good, that was what she wanted.

'You don't know me. Di doesn't either,' he said, drowsed and mesmerised by her fingers washing his hair. 'I only want her to love me.'

'Fat chance of that. You sold her,' Peg said.

He stirred, slumped back.

'It was because her mother was a saint,' Quig said. 'That's what gets in the way. Di made her into a saint. She wasn't.'

'Oh yeah? Mother wasn't a saint, so what? Mine wasn't either.'

She rinsed, vigorously, smoothed on conditioner.

'Her mother weren't a saint. Had a baby long before she met me. Only ever cleaned for rich buggers, probably shagged them all. Liked books and stuff. Way above my mark. Like Di is now. She made me feel small. Couldn't love them, made me feel small. Nothing I could do for either of them. They didn't need me.'

You self-pitying old shit. You're just like my dad.

She hoiked him upright in the chair so fast he was almost awake. Smiling, before his eyes clouded over his smile and tears leaked out of the corner of his eyes. She wanted to steer him towards the blow dryer and blast it in his eyes. Same old story with lousy dads, just like hers. Nobody understands me, blah, blah, shit. I'm bad because somebody else was so much better and I couldn't keep up.

'Oh yeah. So when they don't understand you, you hit them, right? That's what you do when someone doesn't appreciate you, right?'

'I done wrong,' he said, not denying it. 'I done ever so wrong. Could never live up to them, see? Always had more words than me. They could talk me down, anytime.'

Peg paused. She knew about that one. Everyone at home had more words at their disposal than she did, although she reckoned she had plenty enough. It softened her, though.

'Had to make a living best way I could, didn't I? So I had to go away and associate' – he pronounced that word with difficulty – 'with not very nice people.'

'You know what you're called?' Peg said, applying yet more conditioner to extend the whole thing. 'You're called the unofficial undertaker. You get rid of dead bodies, all kinds. You get rid of anything dead for whoever asks you as long as they pay.'

'Why not?' he said drowsily. 'Work, isn't it? And the dead don't notice. I've never killed anybody. Shot birds out the sky, but only to eat.'

She watched the tears continue to leak out of his eyes, and began to rinse his hair. Would have been dead long ago if it hadn't been so curly, better than many an old head in this salon. Salon? Yeah. It didn't seem so bad, burying the dead for money; like tidying up. Maybe she was getting hard but if someone had taken her dad away in a box and put him into landfill, well, it wouldn't have been a loss, but maybe better if she'd been adopted at birth. Too much listening to Di. Maybe she should have given her own dad a second chance, maybe she would. And her mother wasn't a saint, either, didn't even seem to have heard of a condom. And she didn't believe this old man. Old men laid it on.

'So what about Di?' Peg asked, admiring the hair which was velvet smooth when wet. She had an almost scientific interest in hair, actually looked forward to drying it and guessing what would happen when she did. 'And let me tell you now,' she added, wrapping a towel round his head – all right it had been used before and was on its way to wash, but never mind – 'I can't stand a man who slags off his wife, especially if she's dead.'

'Not good, is it?' he mumbled. 'No excuse, really. I wouldn't let her go to hospital. Di threw a knife through my leg when I cancelled the ambulance. I left them to it. She died. I went away. I told Ron to pick up my daughter and set her to work. For fuck's sake, she was already good at smashing windows.'

Like listening to a dream sequence, Peg thought. Don't know what to believe and what not. She led him to the blow-drying chair and sat him in it. Rain had started out-side and all the posters on the windows obscured the view of it. Heavy, midsummer rain.

'So what do you want with Di?' she shouted over the sound of the hair dryer.

'I want to make up to her for what I done,' he said. She shut off the dryer in order to hear. His hair, on the first touch, was already springing back into fine, grey curls.

'I wanna be useful, anyway I know how. I want her to know me. I wanna *help*, know what I mean? I'm her dad. She's all I've got. Just want to be included. Don't want anything else.'

His hair rose like a cloud. Sure, he wanted something else, but it didn't matter for the moment. The other agendas didn't matter just now. He was thinking about Di the way she was thinking about her dad. As if. Quig's hair was a halo, and suddenly he looked a bit like a saint in one of Di's art books. Not that he noticed, still talking, still drowsy, not looking.

'I want to help,' he murmured. 'All I want to do is help and make her notice me. I want to make up for the bad I done. I've tried, God knows I've tried, but she won't have it. And I wanted to warn her ... I wanted to warn her there's someone else wanting to steal from her.'

Crying again. This time, it affected Peg because he was looking so much more handsome with his halo of hair. She saw herself in the mirror, standing behind him and thinking what she had wanted to do this last year, since Di sprang her from prison and took her in and made her all right ... ish. Put her on another path, told her she was terrific, even though they didn't know she listened behind doors. She would never forget the way Di stood in front of the door and pretended she wasn't there when the police came to arrest her, willing to go instead; she would never forget the way Jones followed and stayed with her and got her out; she would never forget how they never questioned what she had done. They were all mad in that house. All those pictures, for a start. Old history now, but she still had debts to pay. All those stories about Quig. And wouldn't it be great if she could get them together?

As if. Forget it.

'I came in the night they almost killed her,' he said. 'I saved her.'

'She saved her fucking self,' Peg said, furious again. Then she leant towards him. 'You know what ? I hate a man who slags off his wife for shagging other people before he got his turn. That the best you can do?'

He was suddenly awake, looking at himself in the mirror and noticing his bouncing head of hair.

'Anybody who asks for love, they don't get it,' Peg said. 'You gotta earn it. You haven't. So earn it, that's what I'm doing.'

'Thank you,' he said, suddenly dignified, bowing from the waist and cramming a hat round his big hair.

'Don't do that, you'll ruin it.'

'Thank you,' he said again, keeping the hat on, pointing to the rain on the window.

'If you want to be useful,' Peg yelled, 'deliver the coal or something. Knock on the door like anyone else, instead of coming in sideways.'

He went off into the grey afternoon and the door made a noise behind him. Peg swept up, tidied around, removed every trace of him and wondered, what if?

Bloody rain. She was no longer afraid of walking home, ever since she had friends in this town. It was good. She thought of her dad and how she had wanted to get him together with her mother. Who was 'No saint'.

You old bastard, Quig. Why can't men just say sorry? If her dad had ever said sorry, she'd be in pieces. She might take him in her arms and stab him after, but not if he had hair like that.

When she got indoors, coming in through the back like they all did, although she really preferred the front door and often used it surreptitiously, she smelled nice smells. Jones was around then, and Saul wasn't, because Saul had a thing about garlic and Jones, when he was around, cooked long and slow and whatever he did used lots of tomatoes and the whole thing took ages until it finally turned into

CASTING THE FIRST STONE

what it was going to become. Start from scratch, he said, and she didn't know what scratch meant, apart from an itch. She sniffed the air, took her shoes off and went to put her raincoat on the hook by the disused front door. She had cleaned this place so rigorously, she hated anyone else to get it dirty.

As if.

Little bits of sand and red-coloured hair, unmistakable, as if they'd notice. Just in the area by the front door which swelled in winter and shrank in summer and she was the only person to use. Where she put her coat and no one else did. Never mind. Still thinking, what if she got Di and her dad back together, wouldn't that really be a result?

He couldn't be all bad, that Quig, not with all that hair. Sad, not bad, and thinking of hair, it really did look as if a dog had been in here. Short hairs, it had to be a dog. Oh, God, don't let them get a dog, all that mess. I hate dogs, please don't let it be a dog.

She went upstairs by the back stairs that led from the front door. Took her ages to work out this house, with its two sets of stairs and two doors into almost every room. She popped into the long room, thinking she was going to wear something different for supper and also to see if that damn dog had been in here as well.

Something wrong in this room, something very wrong.

Her phone went. Got a text from Patrick. Coming tomorrow, oh good!

No word from the lad in the town.

Really, Peg thought, I like older men, or boys who are still boys.

CHAPTER EIGHT

Drawing. *In sepia ink, showing an industrial urban scene. A pit in the scene alive with mechanical movement. Earth-moving machinery – some huge, some so much smaller they looked the offspring of the huge – move things around as if to music. Seen from above. Drawing by Patrick.*

Best thing about the platform from where he would leave the next day was the view. Patrick was going to tell Di about it, in case she never noticed. The high-speed train to the coast occupied the same level platforms as the Eurostar to Paris: you ascended by escalator and you got this view through glass to the left, a family of earth-moving animals that thrilled him. Couldn't they have some pictures of that, or at least some drawings? For sure. They would look wonderful by the sea, like the diggers on the beach. He was proud of his own drawings, stuff he had done down there, and here at the station the last time he came back. You know what? Even that weirdo Saul would be interested. Building works were beautiful. Machines had their own faces, and there were no machines in Grandpa's collection.

Yippee, I'm off tomorrow. I wish that man would go. Yabber, yabber, yabber. Patrick's parents' flat was neither small nor big. He could hear people talking in the living room. Yabber yabber, about those two paintings his mum and dad got given by Grandpa. The visitor was leaving.

Dad's old chum, there again.

'Thanks,' Steven said to Edward. 'Nice place you've got. Good to see these paintings again.'

'It's late,' Gayle said in her even tones. 'Next time, we'll call on you, shall we? I'd love to see where you live.'

'We'll call on you,' his dad said. 'When we're round your way.'

'Sure, anytime.'

That man was back for the third time, and they still

didn't like one another, although they laughed a lot as though they did.

Patrick was quietly resentful. Dad had been looking in his room, taken some of the drawings away, never mind, although he wondered why. Taken a drawing he'd made of Di on the beach and given it to the man last time he was here. Snippets of conversation drifted back. Patrick slipped his sketchbook with the drawing of the man into the folder he was taking to show Di. Now he was twelve, he did his own packing and kept it light. Mum really didn't like Di, but no problems about him staying at Grandpa's house, with her and Peg; something he couldn't quite work out. How could his mother send him off to the coast with not always clean clothes and rely on Di to wash them, feed him, send him back fatter and bigger, and not like her? Or maybe, and the thought worried him, his mother was just pleased to be rid of him. Or maybe she was thinking he was better away from Dad.

They were sitting up talking and arguing, nothing new about that. Patrick closed his eyes and wished his father would leave, go away for ever and then there would be no arguments at all. Especially about those two paintings, propped against the wall, wrapped in bubble wrap, taken out, taken away, brought back, wrapped up all the time. What was the point of a wrapped up painting? His father Edward had once asked his opinion, saying, What do you think of these, son? and been enraged when Patrick had said, I don't know why you chose those, there's nicer than them. Dad went ballistic. Don't you know value when you see it? he yelled.

No, I don't.

Hush, Gayle had said.

The flat where they lived was boring, Patrick thought; way too quiet. Or at least it had been, but now everything around it was being dug up for some new development and that was a lot more fun. They were in something called negative equity until all that was done, Dad said. Now he was older, it was more difficult to fold himself behind the white sofa, or hide against the white walls without being noticed, and yet his father did not seem to register how much he had grown. Bonus, not being noticed by Dad.

Peg was going to meet him at the station, she said in a text, though he could easily get from there to the house; he'd done it on his secret, bunking off school missions, years ago. But Peg would come if she could, she said. Got an iPhone, Peg said. Got all these apps, we can look at boats and planes.

Mum and Dad were still arguing.

The man worried him. Why do you have someone in your house when you don't like him and he doesn't like you? Old chums.

And why, last week, were they telling that man about Grandpa's house when they didn't even like him? And how much of this could he tell Di?

Nothing. Best say nothing more than he had already said. He would sleep on it, soon. He was thinking of food. You had to fight for food round here, but there was plenty of food there. That was what made him grow.

'You've been working, I see,' Peg said, coming downstairs waving her flamboyant feather duster which was a joke. 'Moved yourself into the kitchen, I see. Kitchen table's best place for anything, isn't it? Anyway, I've got his room ready. Patrick's coming tomorrow, goody. Oh, hallo, Sarah.'

When did she creep in? Peg was feeling cheeky and she was two vodka tonics up. Got a text from that lad in town.

'Hello, Peg,' Sarah said, cheerfully. 'What do you think of Di's new top? Sexy, hey?'

'Not bad,' Peg said, not looking at clothes. She was looking for resemblances between Di and her father and certainly not finding anything in the hair. Di had crap hair.

Peg was looking at heads and eyes, not clothes, rallied herself to answer. Sarah had fantastic hair, though, a great red mop. Classy clothes, too; the sort that looked like she'd thrown them on. Not like Saul. Whenever Saul appeared, he looked like he'd spent hours in front of a mirror getting everything straight.

'So you're the one who's got her buying clothes, right. Good on you. What's it like having a brother like yours? He's way weird, isn't he?'

Whoops. Shut your mouth. Sarah laughed. They both laughed, and Peg was mightily pleased to have made them laugh.

'Weird?' Sarah said, beaming at her. 'Weird? You got that right. Mad as a snake, more like. Unpredictable. Hey, Peg, if I came in the salon, would you have a go at my hair?'

Peg decided she liked Sarah.

'For sure, I'll have a go at your hair,' she said, flattered to be asked. 'So where is he, that Saul?'

'God knows,' Sarah said. 'I never did. Think he's gone for a teeny little walkabout in London. Man of mystery. A man with several clients.'

She mimicked her brother to affectionate perfection. Peg liked her even more.

The smell of food, now being lifted towards the table by silent Jones, one of his big old stews, was overpowering. He winked at Peg and rolled his eyes, as if they were the only people in the room who understood one another, and then looked towards D, nodding a message to Peg. Peg followed the code and looked at Di. Di was wearing a shirt the colour of emeralds, although a bit grubby with sand, and she looked a treat in it. She was in different leagues in the clothes stakes to Sarah, maybe. Di was never going to look as if she had thrown the thing on. She was always going to look as if she had slept in it.

'They've been talking all evening about clothes and stuff,' Jones said to Peg. 'I'm bored to death. You look really lovely, you do, too.'

'You're not the only one who's noticed,' Peg said, pertly, sitting upright, eating prettily and voraciously. Patrick coming tomorrow, yeah!

Patrick noticed everything.

'Now then,' Sarah was saying, 'I'm guessing Jones here wears the same clothes every day, but he knows what suits him. Isn't that right, Jones?'

'Yeah, right. Something that fits, no fucking buttons, easy to get on and off. I dress to fish. So I can move.'

'Something roomy with big armholes, nothing restricting, loads of space between elbow and armpit, so that whatever you wear doesn't move and lets you move inside it without getting tangled up.'

'Something like that,' Jones said, interested, despite himself. He never thought about it.

'Is there anything you'd really like to wear and never do?'

Jones grinned. 'A pink apron and nothing else,' he said.

'I know the colours,' Di said, 'only I don't know the shapes.'

And they went on and on, about Jones knowing what colours and shapes suited him, Saul's suits and how they were really disguises, and what did anyone do for clothes before there were shops? That was so foreign a notion to Peg, she was too old for this, when had there not been shops? Well, they knew more than she did and all the same, she had the best hair of the lot of them, even Sarah. She finished her plate and listened, and when there was a lull in the conversation, which had moved on to style and whatever, she thought of one of the paintings in the room upstairs and remembered something. Now that man on the wall upstairs had style, he really did. He seemed to flirt with every woman who came into the room.

'So what's happened to the man upstairs then?'

They went on talking, as if she wasn't there, so she said it again.

'What's happened to the man upstairs? Got style, that one. Love him.'

She was giggling, unaware of the silence suddenly surrounding her.

'What man upstairs? There's a man upstairs?' Jones said, rising to his feet.

They weren't understanding her.

'Not a *real* man. Man in a painting. That fella that looks at Madame de Belleroche from the other side of the room. He's gone. Pity. Had his clothes handmade, I'd guess. Lovely hair.'

Di and Jones ran upstairs. Peg and Sarah stared at one another, and then followed, slowly. They found Di staring at a gap on the wall. From the far end of the long room, Madame de Belleroche gazed at the empty space once occupied by her courtier, the Edwardian rogue, slouched languidly in a chair, wearing evening dress with a red cravat, leering nicely at the world over the smoke of his cigar. *Sketch with blurred outlines, maybe study for inclusion in a group portrait*, Di had written in her catalogue. She was trying to be calm and managing it. There was always a logical explanation.

'So,' she said. 'Something seems to have gone.'

'We got pudding downstairs,' Jones said.

'So we have,' Di said lightly. 'And Patrick coming tomorrow.'

They trooped back downstairs, but they could not continue talking about clothes. Di was shaken.

'Saul,' Sarah said. 'When did my dear brother push off?'

'This morning.'

'Right,' Sarah said. 'Leaving a message? Saying when he would be back, stuff like that? No? He never does, does he? It used to irritate the shit out of me.' She turned to Peg. 'He used to use my flat, never knew when he was coming or going.'

'So,' Jones said, 'was anyone else in today? Apart from you and me?'

'Nobody else, for sure. I went back out in the afternoon.'

'Is it valuable, Di? That painting?' This was Sarah.

'No,' Di said. 'Not in money. Anonymous, no signature. Thomas bought it locally, I think, upwards of twenty years ago. I can only date it by the clothes. No one would steal it for value. It was one of Thomas's absolute favourites. Been in a lot of smoky rooms, like the one he was in when somebody sketched him. Always had the theory that it was the same artist who did Madame de Belleroche. Both of them could do with cleaning.'

'Well, that explains that then, doesn't it?' Jones said, briskly. 'You know what Saul's like about cleanliness. Wants everything cleaned up. I reckon he took it up to London. Done that before, hasn't he?'

Di nodded, willing to be persuaded. She remembered the lightness of the frame, its easy portability. And she remembered that Saul had done something of the kind before. He preferred paintings to be cleaner than she did.

Sarah was on her phone. 'No answer,' she said. 'He was always useless at communication.'

'As long as we're sure no one else came in today,' Jones said, serving up a fruit salad and dumping a jug of cream on the table. 'We can skin Saul alive when he gets back. I reckon he's having a joke. Trying to scare you, Di. Remind us all about security.'

'That would be like him,' Sarah said. 'Always was one for the oblique message.'

'And you didn't ask your friend in, I know,' Jones said to Di, carelessly. 'He walked straight on by. Good walker.'

'Oh, what friend?' Sarah said, her red hair glowing.

Needed hedge clippers, Peg thought, crossly; she'd show her. She was the one who'd noticed the missing painting, and yet again, no one was listening to her.

'Surveyor on beach,' Di mumbled. 'Nice man. No, he didn't come in.'

No one else got in today? Peg thought. Only a dog did. Or maybe Di did ask someone in and doesn't want anyone to know. And I don't always lock the front door.

And we got Patrick coming tomorrow. So we won't say anything about anything. Especially the door.

Saul was in London, Pall Mall, standing in front of the bank where Steven lived. Midnight and the traffic clearing, but still busy. It was covered in scaffold, summer repairs to the façade. When he was young, he could have scaled that building.

A man in uniform approached the front door. Saul intercepted him.

'Excuse me, I was looking for Steven Cockerel. Lives on the top floor.'

The man took his headphones out of his ears, squinted down from his great height to Saul's smaller one.

'Only he asked me round,' Saul said, with exaggerated politeness. 'And he doesn't appear to be in.'

'Nothing I can do about that,' the man said. 'And I can't let you in.'

'But you might be able to take a delivery?' Saul said, pointing to the slim, innocuous parcel under his arm, which looked, for all the world, remarkably similar to a drawing wrapped in brown paper. 'He'd be awfully upset if he didn't receive it.'

'One of them, is it? I'll take it inside, only you can't come in.'

'Thank you *so* much,' Saul said and minced away until he rounded the corner and resumed a normal walk.

So, this security guard was used to receiving stuff and taking it in. Even if all he had taken in on this occasion was a small, flat parcel containing fragments of a local newspaper, something useful was established. A line of communication. The man looked pale.

Janek was not feeling well, wanted the lavatory as he so often did. Tried to ignore it. Then he started getting the tremors and tried to remember the routine.

First, go down to the basement. Check the old safe, all that, don't listen out for weird noises. No ghosts down there, really no ghosts. And the man outside said the man inside was out, so no one here. The trembling started. Steve was out, so he had to do the security check, tick the boxes, go downstairs. By himself. He placed the parcel on the floor by the door, slumped down next to it.

Can't face the basements in here today. Can't tell anyone that that man on the top floor does it for me. Goes round, ticks the boxes and gives me back the list. Ghosts down there. Now he's out, I gotta do it, and I'm scared. He wiped sweat from his forehead. So brave outside, so big and yet always so small in here, it's as if I shrink. Don't know what's wrong with me, only I'm ill, gotta pee, oh shit.

Pitter-patter, down the long stairs, the sound of footsteps skipping down three floors, someone whistling, sliding down the banisters and arriving soon. Oh God, the ghosts had moved.

'Hello, old chum. Shall I do the rounds for you?'

'You supposed to be out, man. Someone looking for you.'

'But I'm not out. Hey, what's wrong?'

'Think I'm having a heart attack, man.'

The face before him blurred. It seemed as if the footsteps were pattering away, but they didn't.

Strong, thin arms caught him and broke his fall to the floor, then laid him down gently. A voice in his ear.

'I don't think it's a heart attack, my friend. It's that awful shit you take.'

CHAPTER NINE

Janek opened his eyes to find himself slumped in a chair, facing a picture.

He felt the draught from an open window, cooling his face, and he was realising slowly just where he was. Been here before, last year before the man he called SC moved in; got as far as the front door many a time since, but never into this room, facing this picture high up on the wall, and another one on the floor, like SC was moving stuff round.

How the hell had he got here? He was on another planet, looking at a painting of some old kind of bank manager type from the days when people wore clothes like that. But this old man in the picture had darts stuck into his big tall hat, and one coming out of his nose. It made Janek laugh and laughing restored him.

'That's more like it,' Steven said. 'You got your colour back.'

'What colour was that ever?' Janek said. 'I don't do colour. But I do do clothes when I get the chance.' He squinted at the picture, nodded wisely.

'Art,' he said. 'I gettit. Ironic. The darts make it art. Old man rules the world, doesn't know he's got darts in his hat. Immune to the reaction of the common man.'

'You're looking better,' Steven said.

'What time is it?' Janek said. 'I'm late, shit, I'm late.'

He hauled himself up out of the chair. He hadn't been here long, but long enough to screw up the schedule. He'd been in this man's flat longer than it would have taken to check the premises and tick the boxes, supposed to take ten minutes.

'It's all right, Janek,' Steven said. 'I phoned in and told them I held you up, losing my key. You got time to spare. I said it was my fault.'

'How did you get me upstairs?'

'The service lift. And you weren't having a heart attack. You were having a downer from that stuff you smoke. You've got to knock it off, Janek, it makes you hallucinate. Panic attacks. If you're going to do drugs, do another kind.'

'You don't know . . .' Janek began. Steven had towelled the sweat off him, loosened his uniform tie, made him comfortable. He was embarrassed.

'Yes, I do know,' Steven said. 'I seen City people wreck themselves with junk. You've done steroid overdose, too.'

'I never . . .'

He gave up. SC knew it all. Wasn't going to tell SC about feeling ill and wanting to pee all the time.

'I been there. Uppers and downers. Wanted to be an athlete once. Would have given anything to make me grow. You should test for diabetes, too. You almost wet yourself. Got in the bathroom just in time.'

Shit. Truth was, Steven Cockerel knew a lot more about Janek than the other way round. SC had picked him off the floor twice before, made him talk. Knew about Janek being the boxer with poetry in his soul, with ambitions for the Olympics, ending up a security guard. What that man knew about him and this building would scare the shit out of a ghost. But he still didn't need to pick him up, carry him up to the top floor when he was sick, get him to the lav. Didn't need to give him an alibi. Or maybe he did.

'You know what?' Janek said, standing steadily and extending the hand that Steven did not take. 'You're a kind man. Thanks.'

Steven slapped Janek's enormous paw with his small, girlish fingers, shaking his head and not smiling.

'Don't ever think it, Janek. I'm nothing but self-interest. I don't want you getting sacked and them sending some-one else.'

Cos you got me by the balls, Janek echoed, staring at him. I could throw you through that window and you'd still have me by the balls. He looked down through SC's feet, spotted the other picture propped up by the wall. Young bloke, dressed up. Loved the clothes. What he really wanted was to be a security guard in a Bond Street shop, dressed accordingly. Armani, perhaps.

'So we aren't friends, right?'

'Allies, more like. Not quite the same thing. We look after each other, right? And now, we're going down to the base-ment.'

'What?'

'We're going to go right through this building,' Steven said, 'Yelling our heads off. We gonna kill them demons. You just got to stop being scared of it.'

Down they went, not in the lift, but running down the

stairs; he was speedy, that man. Two doors to the basement levels, both off the grand foyer. Down and down.

Downstairs, lower-ceilinged rooms, but still big rooms, three occupied by huge, freestanding safes made of steel. SC knew his way better than Janek did, and Janek wondered about what he stored down here. Remembered a time when SC had found him spark-out on the carpet, taken the keys, come back with the signed checklist. Even finding a few faults to make it real. *Key to door, left centre needs attention, treated with wd40. Wood cracking on panelling in left basement.* No signs of forced entry, was all they needed to know. Job done. No need to report that SC stored stuff down here. It wasn't thieves the owners worried about, it was squatters.

The rooms were made for gaslight and still badly lit, insofar as there were bright lights and dim ones, leaving lights which blinded and lights that shaded and plenty of dark corners. Not a place for light and life, only for storage. Strange sounds from the ventilation vents in the walls and all this emptiness. SC made him walk all the way round it, isolate the sounds it made, nothing but shifting, humming noises and moving patterns of light. All the same, it felt safer in the foyer, with the chandeliers and the wood panelling and the great high windows lit by street light from outside, blurring the lines of scaffolding.

'Any more rumours of a new tenant?' Steven asked.

'Only like I told you. Got two weeks of doing windows and stuff, and then they'll go big on it. Look it up on the website. Art installations, big sculpture things, art events, that's what they want. That wouldn't be you, would it? That what you want? You liking art and all?'

'There still won't be ghosts here, Janek. Squatters, maybe. That's the fear.'

'Same thing, maybe,' Janek said. 'But those ghosts, I bring them in with me. Got them in my head.'

'Dump them at the door. Stop inhaling them,' Steven said, roughly.

'What are you like, man?' Janek said, as they stood in the foyer and he handed SC the parcel he had dropped.

'As honest as the next man,' Steven Cockerel said, making a mock bow. 'Which doesn't say much.'

'Too right.'

Janek was thinking of the portrait upstairs, with the darts in the hat. And the stuff that SC stored down here and didn't want anyone to see. Fine by him.

'Gonna be a lot more people in and out of here while they do these building works,' he said. 'They got to get at windows. A whole team coming in and out.'

158

'Yes, I know,' Steven said. 'But not at night. See you tomorrow.'

'That parcel's for you, sir,' Janek said. 'Tall, skinny man left it for you. Shifty fella, nice clothes, though.'

Back in his own bank chambers, Steven Cockerel paused to collect a small brandy, and then resumed his quiet contemplation, not of the rich old grandee with the darts in his hat but of the small painting on the floor.

Why on earth had he done it? Why, when that dog who had adopted him and whose name he had never known, careered back up the beach and hurled itself across the road at that front door, had he followed, put his shoulder against the door and gone in? He supposed it was because he could. He could always blame it on the dog. He had already lost the dog once, as well as his scarf. Maybe the dog he had called Grace, without even knowing if it had a name, sensed that there was food within the big house, and by that time of day, even that crazy animal craved lunch. Maybe he had been hungry himself.

About midday when it happened, three hours after he had met Di at the far end of the beach. He had walked on, towards his non-mother's house, got near, turned back until he was passing the house again, planning to abandon the dog, collect his car. He could blame the dog. He could blame the owner of the house for assuming that a sticking door was impregnable. He would blame old chum Edward for suggesting the idea in the first place. *Can't go back there myself, old chum, but you could. Here's a map. Here's a drawing of the widow. Don't have photos.*

Don't you know, Edward, old chum, that I already knew that house, although truth to tell I had forgotten about it for a few years. But I remembered it; I even remembered that painting. Don't you know that Mummy and Daddy used to take me for tea with Thomas, that nice man who loved children and spoke to me as if I were a grown-up? And don't you know that darling Mummy, who isn't my mummy, but never told me so, leaves me messages, talking about the place. Didn't need you, Edward, old chum; it needed memories and my loving mother, Granta. Time to talk to Mummy. He looked towards the phone, thinking, why not now? Then remembered that not everyone had his nocturnal habits. Granta would not appreciate it, even if there were already three messages on his landline from her and he had not replied to any communication from her for two years.

He sat down suddenly, forgetting the succeeding hours

160

in what had been a very long day, forgetting the driving back to London, Edward, Janek, focusing on the moment, overwhelmed by what he had done.

It had never been his intention: he had not even contemplated it. He had only got as far as exploring the terrain and maybe seeing if there was a way to sidle up to a rich young widow, who, as described by Mummy, was plain and insecure and did not know the value of what she had. Rich *old* widows were more his line. It wasn't *him* who had gone upstairs in that old house, entered that room, looked at this amused young man on the wall, lounging in evening dress, flaunting a cigarette, looking like an elegant version of Oscar Wilde with great long legs. Rich, insouciant, elegant and amused, with the only real flash of colour about him being the red cravat dripping from a top pocket, not caring if anyone noticed him or not, but still the whole centre of attention. Soft, dancing slippers on his feet, one long leg crossed over the other, the foot on the floor tapping to some hidden music. It could not have been *him* who stroked the surface of the thing, only realising how light it was as he lifted it off the wall. It was another person entirely; it was not him. It was another person, wearing that black and white scarf he had lost on the beach. Someone else had crossed that Rubicon and become an outright thief. Someone else had merely delivered the painting into his hands, but then he would not have felt this high.

The cavalier was going to have to go down into the bank's basement, but not yet. He belonged upstairs with the seascapes, not down there with the investments, because he really belonged. He was owned and as if known for years.

I wish I was you, Steven said to the young man. Maybe I was seduced by your clothes.

Diana Porteous is not as described. I did not expect to find her half as elegant, but then, she is part of my larger mission. *Her mother once worked for my father.* How long will it take her to notice a missing painting among so many? Oh, Diana, I am going mad.

Three in the morning. Good time to look at the markets.

Art installations in the foyer. Well, well.

A thief. It was addictive. He knew he would always remember the moment of fleeing the house, triumphant, and knew, like the boy discovering masturbation, that he was going to do it again.

Shame he had lost his scarf. Mummy had given it to him. That man in the picture would have despised it. There

162

was such triumph in this long day. Now, he said to the cavalier, let's hang you where you belong. Where do you want to go? You're mine.

Peg met Patrick off the train. High speed half the way, low speed for the three stations to here. Big hugs.

'Gotta tell you, sweetheart, we're all in trouble. And it's going to rain. And there's this dog hanging around. And Di's gone all serious. Hey, you've grown again.'

'Have, haven't I? What kind of dog?'

'Don't know, never seen it. Thought we might walk round the long way. You gotta see the beach.'

'No more diggers?'

'No,' Peg said. 'None of them. But they might come back.'

'Why?' He was skipping along.

'Cos they did it all wrong. Might have to do it again.'

Got them by the balls. That was the trouble. Jones had a theory about why Patrick was allowed to stay as often as he did. Not for his own good, but because it gave them a spy in the camp. Blackmail worked both ways, Jones reckoned, especially where love was involved. So you limited what you said around that boy, who had eyes like a hawk, and he limited what he said, too. It just wasn't a good time for him to be there, was all, because as sure as eggs were eggs, someone had got in the day before and stolen a painting. Wasn't fucking Saul taking it away.

That much had been clear by breakfast time. Jones had thought of it in the middle of the night. Gone down in the morning, tested that old front door which stuck so badly in winter, it may as well have been locked and barred and they never used it. Something he'd been meaning to fix, a reminder of how lax they'd all got about security as soon as the danger seemed over. The door swelled in winter, which meant it shrank right back in summer, and now without the chain to hold it closed, could have blown open anytime. The chain was off and Jones knew that Peg sometimes used that door when she snuck in late at night. Both she and Di had this hatred of locked doors. Shit.

That Sarah was in the kitchen, sitting with a cup of tea in one hand and her phone in the other. He was glad she had stayed the night, glad she and Di had stayed up, talking. Also glad she was coming back later to meet Patrick; glad that there was someone else who knew the whole story. She shook her head at him, waved the phone.

'Saul didn't take that picture away for cleaning,' she said.

'Tell me news. How comes he answers his phone to you and not to anyone else?'

'I'm his sister, I've got the code. I can sometimes scare him.'

Jones could see that. She put down the cup, elegantly.

'So,' she said, 'that picture was removed, yesterday.'

'Could have been you,' he said.

'Yes,' she said, unoffended by the insinuation. 'I could have stashed it away, but I didn't. I'm not a collector, you see. I don't collect anything.'

'Sorry,' Jones said.

'Don't be.'

There was an easy silence.

'So who?' Di said, from the door.

'Don't know,' Jones said. 'All I know is that all I've gotta do today is fix that door.'

And not tell on Peg.

'And I shall put something else up there to replace the cavalier,' Di said, 'before Patrick gets here. And then we'll behave as normal.'

Sarah had gone by the time Patrick stormed in the back door, smelled the smells and almost clapped his hands. Peg whisked his bag away.

'Hello, boy,' Jones said. 'Gonna rain later, right? Better get out on that beach soonest.'

'Dead right,' said Di.

'Yup. I got my bathers on already.'

He plucked at the elasticated waist of his scruffy track-suit bottoms to show a bright pair of trunks underneath.

'I'm coming too,' Peg said. 'Patrick's going to teach me how to float.'

'I'm gonna drown you,' Patrick said, growling at her.

'And I'll fix that door,' said Jones.

It was hot, coming on to the last of the hot days.

To think Patrick had once been afraid of the waves, and was now drawn to them. He had his grandfather's genes, Di thought as she watched him plunge into the water. Thomas needed immersion in the sea like he needed air: he could be clumsy on land, but free in the water. Patrick was the same, worryingly fearless, while on this particular morning it was she who needed the water more than anyone. It might soothe the terrible, quiet anger that gripped her. She was angry with herself; angry that because of this, they could no longer live the way they had, so carelessly. She had always wanted the house to be open. And she thought she knew who it was. Dear father, dear old Quig, telling her something. See how easy it is to steal, girl? He would steal and hold his prize to ransom, show her how easy it was to penetrate her flimsy walls. It had to be Quig, forcing her hand to make her let him help. Stealing not for value, but taking away something he would guess she particularly loved. She wanted it to be him.

She was out of the water first, sitting in the midst of scattered driftwood, fingering a stone. The chill of the water had not diluted the anger. She held these paintings in trust, and she had betrayed that trust. The sight of Patrick playing in the water with Peg, pushing and splashing like puppies, such a lovely childish flirtation, such screaming, mitigated self-castigation a little. She closed her eyes. Only Patrick could get Peg to play in water.

Then there were shriller screams, not screams for the sake of screaming. Peg screaming in fear, Patrick with joy. The sound of a dog barking. Di shot to her feet. There it was, that great daft dog, running along the shoreline, barking at the children, wanting to join in, still afraid of braving the smallest of waves. They didn't know that; the dog might look as menacing to them as it had to her in the early hours of yesterday. It was afraid of waves; they were afraid of it. Di picked up a piece of driftwood, threw it. Almost before it had left her hand, the dog seemed to sense it, turn round, follow it and lollop after it parallel with the waves.

Grace brought the stick back, so fragile a piece of wood it crumbled in her jaws while she stood there, panting. Di grabbed hold of her ears, letting those in the water see how daft and harmless an animal it was. The hound dropped the stick. She felt for the collar round its neck, found a medallion bearing the legend *My name is Teeny*. The dog whined and protested. She fondled its ears, sandy and silky at the same time, tried again, but the dog pulled away, sniffing at the beach bag and the driftwood, looking for food.

'Teeny?' Di said. 'Not Grace?'

'Come back,' Patrick yelled from the water. 'Come back!'

The rusty dog, following some unknown trail, raised its nose and lumbered off, gathering speed until it was running away.

'That dog scared me.' Peg was panting and trembling as she came back up the beach, hating the stones. 'Looked like it wanted to eat us alive.'

The dog was a dot in the distance, growing smaller.

'I wasn't scared,' Patrick wailed. 'Why did it run away? Did I scare it away? Didn't it like me?'

All his raw insecurity was written on his face, as if he had lost something precious. *Why did she run away? Was it me?*

'Look,' Di said, pointing to the darkening sky. 'It's

168

going to rain. That's why it ran away. Going home for food time, that's why. Same for us, right?'

The afternoon waned into a haze of food and wet rain against windows. There was a game of hide and seek, a cooking lesson, an eating competition, lots of stuff, and still Patrick thought about the dog.

'Could you,' Patrick said, 'have a dog that lived in the cellar? Came in when it wanted, went away when it wanted? Like people did when Grandpa lived here.'

Di mourned those days, when she left the basement accessible enough for anyone to crawl in and find shelter. She wanted it to be like that again, to go back to the days when she was not haunted by the existence of bones.

'Yes, I expect we could. Only I'd rather it lived upstairs and came to supper every night. Breakfast, even.'

'That would be better,' he said, gravely. 'Can I show you my drawings now?'

Sarah had come back, sailing in as if she was at home, part of the furniture. Patrick was introduced and scarcely noticed her apart from the way she looked, taking an interest, not interfering, and full of colour.

'Can I look too?' she asked.

Oh, how Di hoped he would persist with this passion for drawing whatever he saw, with such innate skill, such mischief and curiosity. And yet not be bound down and rendered captive. The folder was unfolded, diffidently, Patrick explaining he was going to leave it here, if she didn't mind. Start a new one, because Dad took stuff. He was embarrassed by praise, but he did want someone to notice and was gratified when they did. Two women, looking at his work, Jones hovering.

He had drawn the digging machines as if they were a tribe of animals, full of movement, each with its own, peculiar expression and determination. He drew his mother and father, sitting, looking at the TV. He drew tables and chairs from underneath. He drew people in school; he could capture movement; he drew the washing machine as if it was a friend. He had an uncanny knack of capturing the likeness of things animate and inanimate.

It was a fine line to follow, whether to praise him so much that he thought there was nothing else he might be good at, or praise so mildly, that he warmed to praise and could still have the alternative of driving a truck for a living. Best thing to do for a happy life was be a plumber, a fixer. Di wished she was.

'And who's this?' Di asked as they sat together looking at the folder. A face emerged from it, sketched in a few lines, seen in profile from the other side of a room. A floppy black and white scarf round the neck to go with the floppy hair.

'Oh that? That's Dad's old chum. I told you.'

'I like that,' Sarah said. 'Can I make a copy of that?'

Di found herself looking at the face of the man on the beach. A face seen mainly in profile, immediately familiar. Someone she had liked.

Patrick looked round for Peg, who got bored by this stuff, but it was Saturday night and she was gone. Nobody needed her this evening.

They still needed her though, you bet they did. Even if Jones had gone all sarcastic on her and said, this time, why don't you come back in the same way as everyone else and not leave the chain off the fucking front door? Fuck off, Jones. I'm the one who fixes things.

This was a town of many pubs, stretched out along the coast and way inland. Peg reckoned she knew this town better than most after a year of exploring. She hurried on, from one pub to the other, guessing, listening to Monica's hints about where Quig might be. Holed up in a pub somewhere, dossing in a back room, maybe, Quig would be in the pub most frequented by the young, who would take no interest in him, not even bother avoiding him. Peg found him in the last one of ten, saw the hair. She was angry, angrier still when he did not recognise her, looked up at her standing over him in the corner he occupied with a pint glass in front of him.

'Buy you a drink?'

'Yeah, double vodka.'

He raised a hand, showing three fingers, the other hand in a V. Triple vodka, tab behind the bar. Coke on the side.

'You stinky old bastard,' she hissed. 'I wash your hair and you get me right in trouble. Don't tell me it wasn't you who came in and stole that fucking painting. You know the way in and out, right?'

'Don't know what you're talking about.'

The drink went down too fast, even for Peg, who had practice.

'I never did that what you said,' he said, turning his bright blue eyes on her and then turning them away. 'It's not what I do. See, I never had the nerve. I ain't a fucking thief and what would I do with a painting?'

He returned to his pint, delicately. It might have lasted for a while.

'All I do is bury stuff,' he said. 'Other people do the stealing. Mind you, I might do it too, if I was paid. Yeah, I might, if I was paid in advance.'

'It's gotta be you,' Peg said. 'You and some fucking red-haired dog. You got in with the dog, the dog took you in, and I'm blamed. You got in with that dog.'

'Did I just? Red-haired dog? Oh, yes, I know that dog, I got business with that dog. Don't you like it?'

The vodka was gone, the second glass arrived. Peg felt tearful. She was forgetting the mission, to make him confess, make everything right. Pay her debts, be able to say, don't worry about the bones. She remembered that rabid, barking dog running up and down the shoreline, shuddered.

'What's the matter, girl?' he asked, patting her hand, slurring his own words only a little.

'Bloody dog,' she said, shivering. The dog, all dogs, haunted her. 'I was frightened of the dog. Don't want it in the house. It was going to chase me and bite me. In the throat, that's what they do. Got a scar from a dog,' she mumbled.

Thinking at the same time, why on earth were they talking about a dog?

He patted her hand again, like a nice uncle, turning upon her his bright blue eyes, just like Di's.

'I only want to help,' he said, from his near distance. 'Don't know how, but I can sure as hell do something about the dog.'

He picked up an imaginary rifle, took aim at the furthest wall, pulled the trigger.

'Blam, blam,' he murmured. 'Can always sort out a dog. Not a daughter, though. And I don't steal anything, paintings, never, but I might know who does.'

He began humming to himself, following his own tune. Peg regretted being where she was, regretted telling him that something had been stolen from his daughter's house; horribly aware that she was making things worse, not better. He smiled at her, which was unnerving, leaned in close towards her, patting her bare knee.

'Next time, little lady, tell that daughter of mine to come herself and not send the messenger girl. Lovely though you are. 'Scuse me, gotta go for a pee. But you been good to me. Don't worry about no dog, I'll see to that for you.'

Quig disappeared behind the bar. Peg waited for ten minutes and he never came back.

Someone else came over. Young.

'Buy you a drink?'

She shrugged. It wasn't the person she wanted, but why not?

174

CHAPTER TEN

Picture. *A rainy day, feeling like Sunday morning. Fishermen on the pier. An old man teaching a young one how to fish.*

A dismal morning, with rain and the feeling as if summer was closing in.

Jones said to Patrick, 'We've had enough of women, son. Let them do the cooking and we'll go out fishing. Man's work, isn't it?'

Patrick nodded, enthusiastically. Breakfast was in the course of digestion, Sunday lunch was too far away, and while he knew the tension in the house was nothing to do with him, he was still aware of it. And yeah, he loved Jones and the way he never talked down, and teased him just a bit but not too much, and yeah, there was a lot to be said about having too much of being fussed over by women. The evening before had not been a spectacular success after he'd shown his folder to Di; she didn't seem interested in the diggers. He didn't mind. But then Jones had had words with Peg, ticked her off about something, and that really upset her and Di had been cross with Jones for doing that and he knew they weren't all saying what they wanted to say to one another because he was there. And Peg and Di kept fussing over him to make sure he didn't notice, so he pretended he didn't. You can leave me alone, he wanted to say. Sometimes I like it.

So when something crashed in the kitchen in the morning, and he heard Jones yell, 'Women, bloody women!' he thought he knew what he meant. And then when Jones dropped his huge hand on Patrick's shoulder in a gesture of solidarity, and said, Come on, tall man, let's go fishing, he was delighted. There was nothing better to do in the rain, and he was going home tomorrow.

What he really wanted to do was to catch fish from a

boat, like the ones he could see from the window with their following crowds of gulls, but that was a different thing, Jones said. Nets and stuff, and the gulls hovering after a catch drove a man mad; they wouldn't leave you alone. Better from the pier. The pier lets you get a line out far enough into the sea to catch serious fish.

Men and boys on the pier, a good day for fishing. First you've got to pick your day, Jones said. And your time of year, and the right side of the pier for the tide. Otherwise you can fish for ever and catch nothing. Jones had armed Patrick with waterproofs, a little too big, perhaps, but authentic enough to pass muster on the pier because it came from the local fishing tackle shop, was cheap and melded in with the predominant yellow from the same source that most of them wore. The pier was not about well-fitting clothes or anything subtle. Look at those turn-stones, Jones said, pointing out the little brown, grey, white birds that ran around nimbly, flew out of the way of feet, perched on the railings as fearless of human beings as they were of the wind and the sea. Patrick would have liked to be like them, too.

It was different going on the pier with Jones, and Patrick had to admit it was better than going with Di. Di did not belong here, while Jones did, and so did anybody who came along with Jones. Those short grunts of friendly recognition, 'Lo, Jones, who's this? Pat. Hello, Pat, what you after? There were lockers at the far end of the pier on the lower platform, and that was real man's territory. Someone loaned Patrick a rod fit, as they said, for a smaller young man. It felt light and easy in his hand.

This is what you do, and this, and this. You take up your station; look, there's room right at the end. It's the casting that's the difficult bit. Then you anchor your rod and you wait. I forgot to tell you, Pat, what this is mainly about; it's about waiting. That's why I said bring your sketchbook. They won't mind if you draw them. No one minds what you do down here. Now, if you drew a picture of Stan over there holding a fish, he'd be your friend for life. Never catches anything. He's here to get away from the women. Like us, hey.

So Patrick waited in his waterproofs, glad not to talk, glad to sit and guard his own junior rod, and be left alone. He thought that, apart from the beach on a good day, this was the nearest thing to heaven. Jones handed him binoculars. No, he said, I want to see what I can see with my own eyes.

So what can you see? Your own eyes are never good enough.

I can see waves breaking out there, look, right on the horizon. What's that?

That's the shipwreck sands, young man. Big old graveyard. A beach in the middle of the sea. Miles of sands and seas and wrecks.

Can we go there? Please can we go? I really, really want to go.

His request was met by silence. Jones had a catch on his line, drew up a pile of seaweed. Patrick's line was still. Nothing mattered, nothing at all. He drew out his sketchbook, turned away from the sea, and drew Stan without a fish. Then turned back to find those distant waves, breaking against a promised land, were now invisible. Both lines were still; the rain fell, making it a good time for talking.

'So how's it all going at home?' Jones asked over the sounds of the sea. He was on his own fishing expedition, but never mind. The boy might drop the sort of hint he never would do to Di, because there was no conflict of loyalties with Jones and men talked better when they were doing something else.

'It's OK, I suppose,' Patrick said. 'Only they haven't got enough money. And Mum and Dad argue, a lot.'

'Reckon most mums and dads do, sometimes. Depends what they argue about.'

'Paintings,' Patrick said, looking hard at his line. Had it actually moved? No, it was still again. 'They argue about those paintings Grandpa left for them and they can't sell them for the right money.'

'Do they really?' Jones said. 'Well, we all know a man who can help them with that, don't we? Saul would tell them what to do to get the best price.'

The pier was such a good place to teach a junior how to fish. Nor was this a squeamish boy; he would know that when you caught a fish you had to kill it.

'Yes,' Patrick said. 'They should have asked Saul but they didn't. They hate Saul, don't know why. Mummy says that if they'd done exactly what Saul told them to do in the first place, it would have been all right. Perhaps that's why they hate him. Still, Daddy's old chum's going to help. Then they'll have some money and be happy.'

'Tell your dad to go back to Saul,' Jones said. 'Saul doesn't care about being hated – he loves it, and he'll do the job.'

They'll never be happy, not them, Jones thought, realising at the same time that enough was enough. Don't push it.

'Can't see Saul out fishing, can you?' Jones said.

'Wouldn't be seen dead in yellow clothes, would he?'

Both of them giggled. Not a good day for fishing, but a good one for learning to fish.

'Christ, we'll be late,' Jones said. 'And the women'll nag.'

They had been at the furthest end of the pier, facing head-on into the sea. The rain was gentle but relentless all the same. Patrick did not know that he was in the middle of a growth spurt, only knew that his hunger was ever present. His body was not quite his own and he was suddenly wobbly with longing for the promised Sunday lunch. They walked back down the pier, Patrick too old and too tall to hold Jones's hand, although wanting to, touching his elbow instead.

'How do you get to those sands?' Patrick said, pointing back to the horizon. 'Do you ever go there?'

'No,' Jones said. 'But I might have to go soon.'

Patrick forgot about it, kept pausing to clutch at the railing and look over the side at the beach as they moved from being over the sea to being over land. He was saying to Jones, could you catch fish with stones, I bet Di could catch fish with stones.

'You mean throwing stones into water, and hitting them on the head?' Jones said. 'Good idea, wouldn't work. Stone loses all power as soon as it hits the water, see? Stop·

a minute, try these bins. Look, see? You can see home from here. This is how you focus. You got better eyes than me, son, but never go without your bins. Here, try.'

Patrick was clumsy with the small binoculars. There was a knack. He focused on the house where food awaited, and then, getting the hang of it, on to the distance of the beach.

'There's that dog,' he said.

'What dog?'

'The dog that got into the house and stole the painting. That's what you were cross with Peg about, right?'

'You do stitch things together, Pat, don't you? You got ears all over your head, young man. We'll make a fisherman out of you yet. You have to learn to listen to fish.'

'Oh yeah? What do they say?'

'They say, catch me if you can.'

Jones put his arm around him and it was fine to snuggle against him as long as they were both wet. It was what he craved. Peg's bosom, Di's understanding and a man's respect. He could see the dog better without binoculars, running closer and running away.

'There it is again. That dog. It's that one, there. Rusty red colour.'

'Hey,' Jones yelled to the man in the office at the end of the pier, 'anyone know anything about that dog?'

'It's feral, innit?' someone said. 'Been on the loose these last two weeks. Roams around, goes with anybody. Old man Ferris's dog, and he died. Can't catch it.'

'Poor dog,' Patrick said.

'I'll find it for you,' Jones said.

'And put it in the basement for the next time I come? And can we go out to those sands?'

'You don't ask much, do you?'

They plodded home, refreshed, pleased with one another.

Two miles down the coast, Sarah got herself into Granta's house. No doubt about it, the old woman had been avoiding her these last days, ever since the last, late-night gin and confessions. Normally, Granta knew no boundaries. She would come round late at night, or call if she fancied a chat, and if they did not see one another, she would text. She was addicted to the mobile phone which Sarah had taught her to use, and equally addicted to her laptop which Sarah had also taught her to use, dragging her kicking and screaming into the twenty-first century and making her an insistent communicator. She boasted about her facility with email and eBay, but what she really did on her laptop was kept secret. Her silence was suspicious, and when Granta went silent, it meant she was either sulking or hiding something. Sarah suspected the latter and apart from that, something was nagging, call it a hunch, a slow-burning conviction that the painting stolen from Di's house and the silence of Granta were somehow connected. And as soon as she had seen the drawing done by Patrick, she thought it even more. Something silly, like the scarf thing round the neck of the drawing, hatched in by soft pencil in black and white stripes, like Granta's favourite dress. A silly connection, a memory of photos of Granta's husband on her sideboard, dressed like the member of some club that would never have him, a persistent wearer of cravats. Sarah did not like cravats.

Which was why she was entering Granta's house, without an invitation, on Sunday morning, when other people were out fishing and the burghers of this small village nestling beneath the cliffs, two miles from the big house of Thomas Porteous, were going to church. There were no big houses here, only quaint ones in the main street, and a sprawl of new developments going uphill, despite which, it was still a place where you could leave your house unlocked, for a while at least, certainly when you went to church, which Granta unfailingly did. Whether this was to pray, either for blessings or forgiveness, or act Lady Bountiful, Sarah neither knew nor cared. I'm not a nice woman, Granta often said. That's all right, Sarah said. I don't like people for their virtues. You can be as nasty as you like, and I'll still like you, but not when you are lying to me about something.

The door was locked. Sarah used her own key, calling out as she went in. She was not a burglar, simply a pragmatist. If she wanted to find out something, she took the quickest way. She had her copy of the picture Patrick had drawn of his dad's old chum. She did not believe that Granta did not have a photo of her adopted son and the hunch was telling her that the two were the same person. A foolish hunch, but prevalent.

There were signs of distress in Granta's living room. Disarray, as if some animal had been wandering around, knocking things over. Nothing too unusual; Granta was not a tidy person and relied on her long-suffering cleaner to restore order every Monday. There was the laptop, winking away on the desk – Granta never turned it off – and the mobile phone by the side. Inseparable as she was from it, Granta would never have taken her phone to church. Sarah started with the laptop. She knew the password: she had installed it. EMAILS SENT.

Granta emailed her adopted son on a regular basis. In fact, most of her emails were to him, over weeks, if not months. Or at least to someone of his name, maybe a fantasy man addressed as 'Son'. None of the messages were returned. Maybe they went into that place in the sky where unreturned emails were sent.

> Remember the sea, remember the times when you liked it here? Remember Thomas and his paintings? Well, I went there the other day. There are all the paintings in the world. Funny little drab woman, that widow, was I ever like that?

No reply, no reply, no reply.

> Anyway, come home and I'll introduce you. You can have all the paintings in the world.

Then, an angrier succession of communications.

> I told them about you, they'll come and find you. I told them you stole my paintings and they're strong, they know you're a thief.

186

Sarah turned to the mobile phone. Messages. Granta did not know how to delete; there was a history of her life in here. One text at the top. No abbreviations.

> Dear mother. If you've put the hounds of hell on me, I'll send them back. The parcel was from you, I presume. Old newspaper, why? Not nice. If you had not refused to tell me who my real mother was, I might not want to strangle you.

Bastard. Calmly, Sarah noted it down. Looked at the clock on the wall. An old electronic clock from the fifties, pleasing shape, paused to think that she liked things with a purpose, rather than things that merely hung on a wall. She explored further, finding Granta's filing cabinet. In here, numerous photos of her son, Steven. She compared boyhood shots to the drawing and admired the drawing all the more. The man had not changed. The drawing told more than the photos. He had not been the God-like boy Granta had described, and he was not a God-like man, especially with a scarf.

She made notes and made coffee. Used Granta's mobile to phone her brother Saul, speaking quietly and at length. Lit a cigarette and waited for Granta to return. Thinking.

So, the man with whom Di had walked with such enjoyment, the one who she had liked, was Granta's son. Who knew all about her and the collection in advance, because his mother had told him. And Granta's tale of wanting back stolen pictures was a double-edged lure. She might have believed it first off, until she had realised there was another reason to bring Steven back.

Time passed and was not wasted.

Sounds in the single street outside – the faithful returned from church, more going uphill than down, only twenty of them and sounding like a crowd. How different from Pall Mall. No Granta. Sarah sat there, carefully filing what she had stolen and noted, and waited. No Granta.

A stirring upstairs, a small vibration of the wind against the windows, a hollow stomach, reminded her of where she was and a delayed instinct of what was wrong.

Sarah went up the steep stairs, carrying Granta's mobile, with each step slower.

Granta looked not quite dead, but almost. Her dark eyes gazed from the depths of her frothy bed, her head sunk among pillows. Eyes that were angry but dim, a voice that could still speak, a swollen face and a bruise on her forehead.

'Oh God,' she said. 'It's you. I thought it was . . . now you know. You know it all.'

'I don't know anything,' Sarah said. 'Did he come here? Steven?'

'No.'

'Did he send someone?'

There was an imperceptible nod and a look of terror.

'An animal, an animal came in here. I fell, it was him and I hid up here. Couldn't come down.'

There was life in her yet and plenty more lies, while she had the odour of illness or injury, Sarah did not know which. There was no disturbance in the room; unlike her downstairs parlour, Granta kept this ruthlessly tidy.

'Don't call the police.'

'Wouldn't dream of it,' Sarah said, and dialled 999 for an ambulance. Granta closed those angry eyes. Her breathing was laboured.

'Why does he hate you so much?' Sarah said.

The eyes opened.

'Because he's his father's son, the animal. Who foisted his bastard on me.'

'And you couldn't tell him who his mother was?'

'Ha, ha. Would you? She was the gentle little cleaning lady. Rogered by my old man. Steven wouldn't like that.'

The eyes closed into silence. The rain fell outside. Pity

overcame all else and while they waited, Sarah fetched water that Granta seemed too weak to drink.

'First time you've missed church in a year,' Sarah said.

There was the ghost of a smile.

'May God forgive me,' Granta murmured.

When the ambulance came and went, carrying her away, Sarah stayed behind. Read all the emails and texts, searched all the corners she could find. Then phoned brother Saul again.

Come home soonest, brother. It seems as if we have, between us, put our friends in danger. We seem to have brought the enemy into our camp. It was supposed to be the other way round. This man is capable of terrorising his mother; he either came in, or sent an alternative animal.

Saul was standing outside that old bank again, in the rain, wearing a Burberry he hated and looking like a prat. Right, that was the time the security man came in and went out, like something going in and out of a cuckoo clock. No telling if it was the same man at night.

The scaffolding hid the contours of the building. Could be useful.

Email communication was never good enough, even if he had known Steven's personal email. A letter was always better in the end.

So he put his invitation through the door.

I am aware of your endeavours, and I believe I might be able to assist.

If only.

A nervous, nasty man, this Steven Cockerel.

CHAPTER ELEVEN

Patrick went back on the Monday.

Tuesday. Hot weather resumed. Jones stayed behind to mind the house, which he refused to leave. All of this going on, and those two bloody women were going shopping. What about thievery and bones in the cellar and a house needing repair, and Peg, staying out late and drinking in the wrong places and coming in the wrong door?

Women.

'All missions must have more than one purpose,' Sarah sang out, halfway down Bond Street. 'Today's the relentless pursuit of beauty and excellence. The conference comes later. We shall worry about nothing and become ladies who lunch. At my expense.'

'How's that?' Di said.

'Because this is my territory, not yours. And because I owe you an apology. My brother and I seemed to have introduced a beast into the camp.'

'I needed a new enemy,' Di said. 'Sharpens the mind. Where do we meet Saul?'

'Somewhere near here.'

They were fresh from the National Gallery, where Di insisted they should revisit en route, this time to look at twentieth-century portraits and get her square on the clothes. She could not bear to be looking at real clothes without looking at paintings first, even though Sarah acknowledged that this was not a buying expedition, rather a day for looking and comparing. For walking into posh shops and trying to work out what each designer was all about, as well as for watching and seeing what other people wore in this part of the world. We are looking at the universal in clothing, Sarah said; we are looking at what might feature in a twenty-first-century painting, even if we might see fit to sneer at it. They strode around like countrywomen with flat-heeled shoes, used to walking everywhere.

No, Bond Street and its environs was not Di's territory, apart from the Fine Art Society, which was the right scale for looking at paintings, feeling more like a fine old house than a museum. Paintings lived in here, gave her ideas, so they had to go in there, too. Not a place where she was familiar, but all the same, this street was delicious and Sarah had the knack of making her forget everything else: she was in her own way as visual as Di was herself, and similarly prone to seeing the ridiculous. Granta would certainly approve, Sarah said. She may be in a parlous state, and she certainly isn't talking, but she would approve. Heart attack and double pneumonia is what Granta had. She was weak but comfortable and a presence on their journey.

'Will Steven come and see her?'

'I gave them his contact numbers. Just as I gave them to you. Lifted from Granta's computer. Now we all have them, don't we?'

'Why are these shops so intimidating?'

'I think you mean vulgar.'

Euro fashion, at dizzying prices. They wandered in and out of Ferragamo, Lauren, Armani, Di in search of colour, Sarah in search of inspiration, designs to replicate, fabric to admire. She was learning to sew. Di looked more at the people, thought she had never seen so many thin people in all her life. The sales assistants were like studies in anorexia-land with the smallest bottoms. By way of contrast there were the security men, huge creatures with mainly black skin, wired for sound like state-of-the-art robots, lurking unsmilingly by doors and wearing beautifully cut suits on powerful torsos.

'Are they guarding the stuff or modelling it?' Di whispered.

'Nice,' Sarah said, admiringly, looking one of them up and down through the window. 'Very nice. Best thing about the shop. But did you see his shoes?'

They met Saul in a similar state of mind, staring through a window, looking at the back of a beige-suited, black-skinned guard with a buzz cut, sniffing at the image like a Sherlock Holmes, whom he slightly resembled today. Loose-waisted trousers with a vintage leather belt, braces and a crumpled linen shirt of pristine white. Loafers, no socks. Not a million miles from his sister's clothes, although more studied for effect.

'Look at him,' Sarah said. 'Bless.'

Di did not feel like blessing Saul. His incessant, manipulative secrecy grated more than ever, as much as his many personas, the several hats he wore, the several clients he had and his endless duplicity. When the three of them sat down together, she could see the resemblance between the siblings, not only in their looks but also their personalities. They were far more systematic than she would ever be, far quicker to judge and condemn, and she loved them both. Sarah and her brother were on their own territory and their faces shone with the joy of intrigue.

'Are you ever coming home, Saul?' Di asked. 'Or should I rent out the room?'

'I am ever attendant upon your affairs,' he said, smiling at a waiter in the Royal Academy restaurant. Di did not like it: it was underground. She wanted a quick bite to eat, information and movement. Instead they were waiting for green soup.

'So where are we up to? Tell us everything.'

'We are pooling our information and assimilating things.'

'Oh, do shut up.'

He smiled on them both, benignly, the two women he loved. That realisation came as a bit of a surprise. He would have killed for either of them, although dying for them was another matter. Since Saul cared more about pictures than anything else, the single fact of having one stolen had driven him to quiet but intense fury.

'Well. I've been away, as you know, contacting clients. Who, as of today, and due to the suggestion of the lovely Patrick, now seem to include Edward.' He nodded to Di, as if to say, well done. 'Who wishes to consult me about the proper way to sell a Fragonard and a Gainsborough. Silly, silly man. Should have asked sooner, rather than bodging it.'

They waited.

'So,' Saul continued, disliking the silence. 'You don't want to hear about Edward and Gayle, I know. You want to know about this bastard, Steven Cockerel, who in all likelihood stole the painting that went missing last week. As if I would have taken it away for cleaning without saying so! As if. But there is a connection with the dreadful Edward. Steven and Edward went to the same school, by gum. When Gayle's paintings, liberated from Di, failed so catastrophically to sell, Steven may well have liaised with an old chum. That's his speciality: he finds people whose auction hopes have been dashed, and are now desperate to sell. Then he screws them into the ground. Anyway, he visits Edward and Gayle. And Patrick drew a picture of him.'

The silence remained. Three bowls of soup were slow to arrive.

'I'll deliver it as a lecture, shall I?' Saul said, looking up at the walls. 'This place was famous for lectures. Like Thomas was.'

'He made it interesting,' Di said. 'He got to the point.

198

And the point is that Edward might have pushed Steven in my direction as a feckless little widow with lots of good stuff to steal or take, and he might have done that long before Granta pointed us in the direction of *him*. Unless that too, was contrived.'

Saul turned to Sarah. 'How is she?'

'Very sick and uncommunicative. You think Edward might have primed Steven about a collection ready to be grabbed? Offered to help him, maybe even give him local contacts.'

Di thought of Quig. And Patrick, bringing news home, answering questions like any good son. Well, that was the price.

'Looks like it.'

'Or Granta did,' Sarah said. 'From her emails, she certainly did. Anything to lure him to her side. First, she threatens him, saying she's hiring someone to come after him and get her paintings back. Then, after she meets Di, sees the house, she thinks, hey, that's an even better way to get him home and put herself back in favour.'

The soup tasted sour. Di shook her head.

'There's more than that,' she said. 'The man I met on the beach, he *knew* the beach. He really was in his own territory, like you are here. He knew what had been done and he knew the coast like he'd been born on it. So, he may be primed by Edward, but where was he born?'

'Birth certificate says here, Granta named as mother. Parish records have him christened in our village when he was three. Granta told me they had a weekend house before Cockerel senior built the new development and they went there for good.'

Sarah stopped, looked warningly at Saul.

'More research required,' Saul said. 'But for the present, does any of this matter? The point is, he has a painting he's stolen from Di, or had stolen from Di, and probably a lot more he's extorted from other people. And he's hiding them in that bank where he lives. So that's where we're going. Tell you more on the way.'

Down Bond Street to Piccadilly, ignoring the jewellery shops. Moving through St James's, down to Jermyn Street, past the back entrance to Fortnum's, noses pressed against windows, what with Di and Saul looking in the galleries, Sarah looking for scarves and Saul also glued to a shop which sold nothing but antique globes. They reached Pall Mall circuitously and crossed the wide road and then stood quietly surveying the grand façade of the bank, obscured by scaffolding and seen through a parade of moving cars.

'Several contacts have been made with Steven Cockerel,' Saul said, reverting to lecture mode. Sarah and Di gathered closer to hear him over the traffic.

'I left him a parcel on Sunday, purporting to come from his mother, just to see if I could get a delivery in. Then I dropped him a letter, offering to be his agent. If he's in touch with Edward, Edward will no doubt vouch for my dubious morals, which should make me appealing to him. I've yet to hear. And I've got maps of the bank.'

Di looked at the building and felt for the stones in her pocket. She felt as if she was a pygmy looking at a giant. Sarah was doing as Sarah did, looking at the workmen on the scaffolding, absorbing as much as she could of what they wore and the size of their legs.

The front door opened and closed. A man in a yellow overall went back in, punching out a code on a panel by the front door. Traffic roared. A window smashing would still attract attention: that sound had a sound entirely its own.

'Thinking of breaking and entering is all premature,' Di said. 'Way too extreme.'

'I wasn't thinking of breaking anything,' Saul said. 'And I was only thinking of entering as a very last resort.'

I liked the man I met on the beach, the very man who might have used a dog to terrorise someone who loved him. Right.

'Isn't it best to befriend the enemy?' Di said. 'Or at least try that first. Like I've done.'

'Like how?'

'I sent him an email, saying if he had the painting, to send it back by courier. No need to reply, just send it back. And then maybe we could meet and discuss our common interests.'

'You are so utterly naive,' Saul laughed, sticking out his hand for a taxi. Time to go home.

'How did you get plans for the bank building?' Sarah asked, ever the researcher.

'Planning applications. Matter of public record. There's been six on this building. Plans on local authority website. Amazing, isn't it? About as secure as a sieve.'

He was terribly pleased with himself.

Good of them to tell me they'll be back late, Jones thought to himself. Nights just beginning to draw in. At least I've made it up with Peg.

That's all right, she said, cheerful as usual, a good-natured girl. Only give me a key to the front door, and I promise I'll be careful. I was daft and you were right. Shouldn't have left that door fit to open, but I'm going to come and go as I please, right? I'm a big girl, now. If I come home pissed, I come home pissed, right? I'll still be at work in the morning.

Big girl, she was, too. Small in height for sure, but big in all the right places.

Right. Only don't be too late. As long as you come home. They both knew there was the odd time when she didn't.

Shuttit, Jones. Give us a kiss.

She'd got harder, Peg. He watched her bounce away down those front steps and sighed. Oh, for being younger than fifty-five. He was in no shape to command a nineteen-year-old who had once adored him. Someone else's turn now, and they better treat her right. What was it like to work like she did, through a hangover? All he could do with a hangover was fish and dream. Caught his best fish that way.

Jones was taking advantage of the absence of everyone to consider things they had chosen to forget. Like the basement. He had no fears of the place, even though it haunted him. He had left Thomas Porteous alone to go down to his basement eleven years ago, left him for good reason, because of that fucking flood which killed that bitch of a wife. Who was old, dry bones, down there, desiccated by salt, packed in silk: the woman liked clothes. If he did nothing else for this household, he would help get rid of those bones. Got old Daniel primed for a trip to the Sands, if that's what Di wanted, the silly woman. Only two or three possible dates in a small fishing boat, one of them coming up soon. Patrick had reminded him. Better make sure they were fit to go. *I must go down to the sea today. The lonely sea and the sky.* All that shit. And besides, old Missus P had to go before they got the builders in.

Sweet smelling down here. A great arched ceiling, fit for a wine cellar, ruined, as Saul would say, by the interruption of a wall which meant the arch somehow stopped while the curve of it went on. Thomas had tanked the basement and made that wall with the door into the space behind, where the old floor went downhill into shingle and the water rose from beneath when the wind drove the tide, as it did, every decade or so. Not since the night of the storm when that woman had fled in there and drowned. Maybe it would never flood again, although he doubted it. Those bones, those damned bones.

He and Saul had packed them up close, stitched into a pristine linen dust sheet, then rewrapped them in a silk cloak from the dressing-up box Thomas kept, so the bones could breathe. Jones was sure no one else had helped: they did it on the night that Edward and Gayle came in, and Edward had almost knocked down that wall. *Dem bones, dem bones, dem bad bones*, he was humming to himself, opening the door the way he knew how. So much tidying up down here since that night when Edward and Gayle got in, he had forgotten how much. He took down a radio and worked with the noise of music, steeling himself to look at the skeleton shroud.

Lights, music. Her cloth coffin was as empty as daylight. The purple cloak left, looking almost the same as it had, but inside it nothing but a small pile of kindling wood. A little litter, maybe, like as if someone had taken a hammer and smashed this desiccated selection to make it smaller. Jones was stunned. Them bones was gone, glory be.

Gone, gone, gone.

Then he thought of Quig. That was what Quig was good at. Quig got rid of bones, got rid of bodies, reduced dead matter to rubble and planted it somewhere. Be it a dog, or dead horse, or a dead cow when you didn't want to call the vet and pay the cost, you called Quig. You wanted an animal shot, you called Quig. Find interesting old bodies in your building site, you called Quig rather than stop work and pay the cost of delay. Famous for it. Worldwide trade. Gotta be Quig. Family disputes, someone already dead and needing illicit burial, you needed quick service Quig. Peg never believed him when he talked about Di's dad. Tell me how he did it, she said, and didn't believe him.

Sticking around, getting older, Quig. No one else could have shifted these bones.

Must have been Quig stole the painting, too. Jones was in such a state of shock, he was upstairs before he knew it, sitting in the kitchen, getting a drink, before sitting down to think.

No, Quig was commission only. Never did a thing without payment upfront.

Unless ... On the second drink, he decided he was going to say nothing about anything. Not until he'd tracked down that bastard Quig.

His ersatz family came in the back.

'You got bones for supper,' he said, and, watching the crestfallen faces of Di and Saul, added, 'Only joking. Eggs on toast OK? You prissy little so and so, Saul my man, where've you been?'

They embraced like long-lost enemies, with real affection.

Di went up to her computer. Waiting for an email in response.

Befriend the enemy. Especially if you liked him and quite understood a thief. And was he a thief? Paying the lowest price you could was not quite theft.

She gazed at the screen, waiting for signs of peace. It was her role in life to be the peacemaker.

So much more logical, Thomas had said. She wished she could talk to him through this screen, but she couldn't.

She thought about the scaffolding round the bank. Yes, she could climb up there. She had done it before, after all.

A long time ago. Another life.

It just needed the right amount of anger.

Chapter Twelve

Picture. *Fishermen on the beach. Black tents and lanterns. A full moon. Anon, circa 1910.*

Peg and Jones were out of sorts again. He was in a bit of a black mood, catching her when she went out in the morning. She was skipping breakfast, and she told him she was going to be out late that night, on account of a bonfire party on the beach. He caught her going out via the front door, and he still didn't like her doing that.

'Peg? When you go to work today, can you ask Monica

if she knows where Di's dad's hanging out? Cos we need to know.'

'Who's *we*? Why's everyone so down on him? Why don't you ask Monica yourself?'

'Not exactly talking much, these days,' Jones mumbled, taken aback and defensive.

'Why don't you grow up? People you've known all your sad life. Thought you and Monica were mates. Grow up. Phone him, he's got a phone, hasn't he?'

Jones lost his temper and grabbed her arm.

'You been talking to him, have you? Don't go near him, girl. Just don't. You been talking to Quig, Di'll chuck you out.'

Her arm was bare and his grasp hurt. She looked down at his hand, locked over her wrist, looked up at him with her bright, bold eyes. He let go of her abruptly, seeing pale, vulnerable, skin, red-varnished nails and a look of scorn.

'Don't touch me, Jones. Go look for him yourself. And Di won't ever chuck me out, she said so.'

'Don't bank on it.'

'So I mustn't go near the bad man, but you'd use me to find out where he is? Get lost.'

'I'm sorry,' he began, but she was gone out that front door and shouting after her would only make it worse. Fuck. Blown it.

No short cuts, Jones, my boy. Gotta spend the day looking for Quig. Start with binoculars on the pier. And why did he think she knew where Quig was? Only that she knew things about this town that he didn't.

A day passed. Lounging around, cataloguing, planning for a future as if there was one. Thinking of alternatives. Saul was pleased to be here. London was where he belonged, but this was his spiritual home because it housed the best private collection he knew of. Which he was destined to protect, bring alive. Preserve from theft, and failed to do so. Why did Steven take *that* painting? Saul was willing Steven Cockerel to think about him, Saul, as much as he, Saul was thinking about Steven. Send us a sign, Steven C.

Why *that* painting?

He was standing in front of the replacement, shaking his head. A beautiful thing he had secured for Thomas, who knew exactly what he wanted: coloured drawing, sketch by Frank Brangwyn, 1905, to be part of a greater design for the Society of Ironmongers. In the words of Di's catalogue: *Two sinuous but sturdy blacksmiths wielding hammers, talking to each other, shirts rolled down round waists, rich, pale torsos. Svelte, rather than massive. Huge feet and boots, rippling muscles. Industrial background; you can smell the smoke of the foundry, feel the heat.* Mayhem in the background. Terrific arms. Men talking and working. Men talk best when working. Brangwyn, a vaunted artist in his time, decorator of buildings, works of his languishing in basements of public collections which had once hailed him. Another kind of theft, Thomas had said.

Saul laughed softly at Di's choice of the replacement for that stolen Edwardian cavalier. The Brangwyn would have fitted anyway as long as this collection was going to be about reviving the forgotten, but it looked as if Di had chosen it purely to appease Madame de Belleroche, so that now, Madame was facing two splendid, bare-chested working men, instead of a single gent in evening dress. She, too, seemed to approve.

But why had Steven Cockerel gone for *that*? Not high value, not a named commodity; would have been extremely valuable if, say, John Singer Sargent had painted it, but he hadn't. No one knew who had, and probably no one ever would. God knows, Saul had tried. But, perhaps Steven did; no, he had no reputation for esoteric knowledge, he was, rather, a cherry-picking opportunist. So why this one? Even in this house, with its superlative stock of paintings bought for quality and joy, he could have done so much better. There were plenty of portable items worth far more, especially in this room. Madame herself, for instance.

Oh, dearie me. The next thought that occurred to Saul worried him more. Supposing the fool had simply fallen in love with it? That made him ten times more dangerous.

He had mentioned it to Di during this waiting, working day. Perhaps, she said, it looked like someone he knew. Perhaps it was a picture of someone he wanted to be.

'I wish he would reply,' she said, looking at her screen. 'Send me a sign.'

'So do I,' Saul said, looking at his. 'What on earth is the matter with Jones?'

Steven Cockerel, sitting in a meeting in the City, found it difficult to concentrate. He wished, sometimes, that he was the kind of Londoner who never wished to be anywhere else than here, and wished he knew who he was. Instead of concentrating on the matter in hand, which was, as it always was, money in all its manifestations, he was thinking of the actual texture of gravel, in context. A company he part-owned, suppliers of stone, shingle, man-made rocks, for construction, for flood defences, shifting stuff from Rotterdam to India and back, were falling foul of their opportunities. Time to pull out of this operation.

Shame, because it was interesting. They were going to the wall, someone said, if you'll excuse the pun. Sell, before anyone else realises, that was the game. There was no sentiment at all, merely a little regret. Done deal, pull the plug on it, just get the money out and move on.

Out in the air, walking fast, he was reflecting on how insecure the world was as soon as you stopped paying attention, because they should have pulled out of this company before and only stayed because of his personal interest. So difficult to know who to trust, but generally speaking, if you trusted implicitly in the inevitability of greed, you got a result. He pulled Saul's handwritten, hand-delivered letter out of his smart case. Greed was the key to the kingdom.

This Saul Blythe sounded greedy and he had nerve. Edward, old chum, said he was the biggest bastard unhung, without specifying why, which coming from Edward was a sterling recommendation. Yes, he would reply to Saul, suggest a meeting and decide for himself. I have several clients, Saul had written in an attractive script. I am exclusive to no one, and I have aided major clients in the direction of major acquisitions. So much said in so few words, Steven admired it. Email and phone provided.

But as for the other missive, the email from Mrs Porteous, Steven was stumped. Where was the greed in here? And how the hell had she found out so swiftly? Was she surrounded by a legion of spies? Motive? Everything that it might or might not be paralysed his brains and prevented any response. Such as, if the picture was hers, why didn't she simply report it stolen? Was that because she couldn't prove it was hers, or did she simply abhor trouble? If he responded to her, he would be making an admission, and he simply did not know what to say. Let her hang about and let her wait. He was never going to give that picture back. It was his, he loved it.

Like Granta's pictures were his by right. So sorry she was ill, but he had sworn, in front of her and behind her back, that he would never see her until she fessed up, rose up out the mountain of her snobbery and told him who his mother really was. She might die before she did so, but that was her choice.

I gave you life, she had said to him. I raised you, fed you, got you taught.

Yes, he said to himself. You did. But you would not give me my identity; you denied me knowledge of my own mother and the brothers and sisters I might have had. That makes me hate you.

He thought of all the people he hated and the none he loved. I am not a nice man, he thought again to himself.

A chill on the shore by evening time, and all this getting less and less of a good idea. Bonfire on the beach, plenty of drink and minimal food. Way to go, only it wasn't. Birthday party of girl who got her hair done in the shop, and her spotty boyfriend and a few others Peg had met in pubs. Really, they were all so soft. It felt as if they were years younger than she was, knew nothing. Words going round her head: *You been talking to Quig, Di'll chuck you out.* And then, Monica's furious response, when she'd asked about Quig, willing to help Jones, after all. You talk to Quig, you're dead in here? Got that?

A long horrible day that went on as badly as it had begun. Now a bonfire, everyone talking nonsense. Teenagers, hey? Not a one of them who'd been to prison and knew what she did. None of them could have done what she had done, none of them worked like she did. The boy she had been texting didn't turn up.

She made them laugh, Peg did, but somehow it wasn't working the other way round. They were just fucking stupid, they couldn't even light a fire, but when they did it went like fury. They'd gathered half the driftwood this end of the beach, along with a lot of household rubbish they shouldn't have been burning. She was never going to get as pissed as this again. It had to stop. It made her as silly as they were.

She was sitting on the landward side of the fire, away from the group and the toxic smoke which made her sneeze, looking up at the stars, awash with disappointment, when Quig came and sat next to her. He appeared out of the black void that was the beach outside the circle of eerie light created by the fire. Drunk as she was herself, she sensed he was drunker.

'What do you want?' she said, looking towards the fire so as not to look at him. He giggled and moved closer.

'Got a nice present for you,' Quig said. 'For being so nice to me. For doing my hair.'

'I don't want anything from you, Mr Quig.'

'Didn't you ask me a favour?' Quig slurred, sounding hurt. 'You wanted rid of that dog. That dog worried you.'

'I never asked you any favours. Go away. You'll scare the kids.'

'I don't scare anyone,' Quig said, sadly. 'Busted flush, me, but I can still kill a dog. Or skin a cat. Specially if it's halfway dead already.'

He belched. 'Was trying to eat a scarf, I finished it off. Didn't even need a gun. Left it for you as a present. You and Di. It was aiming for your house.'

She did not know what he was talking about, only that he was rambling and she could not move her mouth to form an answer. She could simply feel his waning but still real strength and smell his smell. What dog? The one that scared her, the one she'd heard about, running ill and wild? Someone staggered towards the bonfire, threw on what looked like an old curtain and it went up in a whoosh, lighting all the faces.

'Wanted to show you how I could help,' Quig said. 'What I'm good at, getting rid of things.'

'I don't want help.'

'We all need help. When they chuck you out, you'll need help. Anyway, I'm going away. Got a job. You tell them.'

She could see a couple of the youths in the group, eying them up, not liking an old man here; not liking Peg talking to him, wanting a bit of action. Quig saw it too. He got to his feet, grunting, and hobbled away down the beach towards the sea, disappearing into the darkness downwind of the smoke. Peg hauled herself up, tottered away in the opposite direction towards the road and home. Whatever would it be like living in this place if she did not have that to go to and only these half-baked kids for company? She was confused and miserable, thinking of the kind of real man she would like to be with, patting her pockets, glad she had worn a coat, unlike most of the silly kids who were going to perish later, checking she had her phone and her key to the front door, because she didn't want anyone seeing her like this. Don't look at the time.

Jones had fixed the light over the front door. It felt as if it was a kind of welcome and an apology. It came on as she approached and she staggered towards it gratefully. In the pool of light at the bottom of the steps there was a dog with a scarf round its neck, lying on the ground.

Peg tripped over its flank and screamed and screamed.

CHAPTER THIRTEEN

She had been willing Steven Cockerel to send a message in any form. There had been nothing; no delivery, no sign. Instead, there was this macabre delivery of a dead dog, strangled with Steven Cockerel's scarf, as if delivering a gift.

There were two things to be done: first get Peg indoors and warm her because she was cold and weeping. In the late days of August, there was already a fire in the snug next to the kitchen. Saul came down with his battery of unguents and herbal remedies, saying take this, dear, take this and that, until she puked into a basin held for the purpose and began to recover. They were together in this one, she and Saul, suddenly united. Never could stand dogs, dead or alive, Saul said. Did it follow you home? Can't you do better than that?

Oh God, Quig, that bastard. Peg trembled and rambled, naming no names, clutching Di's hand.

'You won't chuck me out, willya, Di? Whatever I done.'

'The very idea. Whoever said such a thing?'

'Even if . . .' *Even if I talked to Quig? Did his hair for him?* She couldn't say it and said instead, 'Even if I get pissed and stay out?'

'Get drunk and hang around with kids? Not a crime.' Di tucked a blanket round her knees.

'I tripped over a dead dog,' Peg murmured, snuggling down. 'Someone said they'd killed it and left it for me.'

'One of those kids you were with?'

'One of them silly kids, yeah. Where are the real men when you need them?'

'Here,' Saul said, and led her away to her bed.

Where was Jones when you needed him? Night fishing.

Di went out to the dog, carrying a flashlight and the blanket she had put round Peg. The dog she knew as Grace had lost the collar that called her something else, and in its place was this black and white bandana wound tight round the neck, as if to throttle it. She sat on the bottom step alongside the body of the dog and stroked its head. Cool to the touch, not cold, long silky ears, the body of it painfully thin with ribs protruding on the rough, visible flank. It had grown a winter coat too early: it was out of sync with the seasons, starving thin, like a racing greyhound. Gingerly, she managed to loosen the scarf. She touched the prominent ribs, patting gently, ready to weep for it. Then it growled, a sick, rumbling sound that rocked her back on her heels with shock. The dog raised its disproportionately large head, attempted to snap, sank back with the effort. She kept the head down with one hand on the neck, stroked the flank with the other. Then took both of her hands away and covered it with the throw. Shush, she said shush. There, there.

She spoke calmly and clearly into her phone; stray dog, badly injured, needs RSPCA. Can you take it indoors, they asked? Yes, but I don't know what do.

It was the same feeling angry frustration with Thomas, and the long months of his illness when she had not known what to do, either. Except to keep him warm and fed. All it needed was warmth. She lifted the dog into her arms. A poor old girl, lighter than a feather, being warmed by touch. It rested easily, coughed, and lay still. Like Thomas, a creature beyond warming, and Di had never been so angry, even then.

It was one o'clock in the morning when Jones came back. He was feeling that he didn't know his own town nearly as well as he had, and it made him defensive. It was as if, in choosing to protect Di and company, he had set himself apart, lost so many of his sources of information, including Monica, who had been invaluable for the gossip. OK, Monica had harboured Quig, and they had fallen out about that, and while she had more than made up for it by taking on Peg, Monica and Jones were distant. He missed her; he missed the old fisherman who had died last winter, and others who trusted him to be what he was, an unofficial outpost of law and order, and he missed his declining contacts with old police colleagues who used to warn him when something was going down. Now they didn't, the old order changing, and the mist around the pier blocked the view. In hours of looking, he had failed to find Quig, or anyone who would talk about Quig, bar a vague suggestion that he might be living out of town on a farm. All he had learned in a lonely day was talk about the dog.

The bones, those missing bones, worried him and haunted him with failure and a sense of ineptitude. Jones felt he was losing his touch, so when he hove in sight of the house and saw a police car at the front door, he broke into a run. History repeating itself; someone being taken away, him failing to prevent it, yet again. But they weren't coming in. Two of them talking to Di on the top step with every sign of respect. And they were only coming to take away a mortally sick dog for delivery to the RSPCA, quicker at that than catching thieves. This was so much better than it might have been, he almost laughed at himself. Almost.

They let him look at the poor, thin beast. Looked bigger and heavier than it was, because of the big head. No gunshot wounds, nothing to indicate assassination. If Quig had tried to kill it, that would be the way. Looked more like it had poisoned itself, eating crap. He knew by now that this dog had been running around for a fortnight, mad as a snake and starving, eluding capture, even getting into houses and gardens. Crazy, sad dog. Better off if it had died, hey? He tried to say as much when they were back indoors.

'Not quite worth crying over, or not for long,' he said to Di, with his inappropriate heartiness. She had been crying copiously and he hadn't found Quig, so this didn't seem a time to mention anything like bones. 'Could have been anyone's doorstep, Di.'

'But the fact of the matter is, it was Di's doorstep,' Saul said, sipping his brandy decorously, sitting far apart from Di who had, after all, been embracing a dog. 'And it was wearing what looks like Steven Cockerel's scarf. Now if that isn't a signal of some sort, I don't know what is. A gesture of contempt, isn't it? Declaration of war, or at least a refusal to surrender. Here I am, this is what I can do.

Meantime, he gets in touch with me, and wants to meet. Adding insult to injury.'

'Oh, come on,' Jones said. 'How would some rich git from London deliver a dying dog?'

'How could a rich businessman walk into a house in the middle of the day and take a painting?' Saul said. 'But he did.'

'Easier than wrestling with a rabid dog and carrying it across a beach.'

'It needn't have been him,' Saul said. 'It could be someone employed for the purpose.'

They were all thinking of Quig.

'Couldn't have been Quig,' Jones said. 'He'd have shot it.'

'He'd do whatever he was asked to if he was paid, right?'

'Either way,' Di said, as coldly angry as he had ever seen her, 'it's got to be a signal. Someone is emphasising a connection. Someone is jeering, making a sick joke designed to scare me, us. Someone's being cruel. What kind of shit punishes a dying animal? Feels to me like a declaration of war. Makes me want to rob a bank and throw stones through windows. Can't sit back and do nothing.'

Jones put his head in his hands.

'Robbing a bank is definitely what I call women's work,' Saul said, perversely pleased by these signs of angry life, liking the idea even if it represented an impossibly illogical leap. 'Needs a feminine touch. Sarah will absolutely adore it.'

The council of war was the next day. Those present, Sarah, Saul, Jones. Peg, with the resilience of youth, had gone to work, bleary eyed but determined, going out the back way, hugging Jones on the way out and laughing off his sympathy. Saul had printed out his official plans of the old London bank. Remarkably detailed. Di was amazed by their availability, had a love of maps and plans: they inspired her with confidence and she was good at memorising them. Anything was possible with a map. Jones was still in a state of shock, wanting to excuse himself from the whole ridiculous thing and go on hunting for Quig, wanted to shout at them about bones, but not daring and strangely mesmerised. Thinking at the same time that if these lunatics were really planning to get inside a bank building in London, well Di was way out of her league. She'd been a good little burglar once, terrific at smashing windows and getting in through small spaces, difficult to catch, but hell, nothing on this scale. That Sarah was another matter: she glowed with confidence in the enterprise. Jones wondered what she had been in her other life and did not care to speculate. Saul had been a thief, too, adept at getting into other people's houses. He was addicted to the roof space, he'd told Jones, and it had always been in an honourable cause, like this. They were all mad. Who was going to let them in, on fucking Pall Mall? Why was Di even contemplating the risk of going back to prison? Anger, sheer anger about that bloody dog, and plenty of other things. She was going to rob a bank because she couldn't stop a dog being hurt, couldn't stop Thomas dying; it was as simple as that. And that Sarah was all for it because she thought that dog had been sent in deliberately to scare her old neighbour into a heart attack, and she wasn't listening either because she was as nuts and irresponsible as her own brother.

Women's work. Maybe yes. That Sarah could talk herself out of anything, and if they were caught in the loop, it would go easier on girls.

'I entirely agree,' Sarah said to her brother. 'This is women's work. Planning, attention to detail, all that. How do we get in? I reckon that's all down to the clothes. All those workmen, wearing yellow with a black logo. So we wear yellow with a black logo. Not unlike that gear they wear on the pier, isn't that right, Jones?'

He nodded, dumbly. What was in it for her? Why should she be so willing to join in this scheme?

'What's in it for you?' he asked.

'Revenge?' she said. 'Remember the original scheme was to get Granta's paintings back? That's what I signed up for. Might make her better if I do. And,' she added, 'I like a challenge.'

Like it? She was loving it, the mad cow.

'Maybe Granta drove Steven mad,' Saul said.

'Meant to tell you,' Jones said, 'something about that Granta. Old lady told me. She ain't that Steven's mother.'

'Our researches,' Saul said, smoothly, nodding to Sarah in a coded communication which the others missed, 'indicate the same. Back to main point,' he continued. 'I was coming down to tell you last night, that I have in fact heard from Mr C. He's taken the bait and wants to meet. So he sends a dying dog to you, and a perfectly comprehensible, polite reply to me. Leaving the time and place to my convenience. So, I suggest I make an arrangement, for dinner or some such, as I would with any client. Once he agrees, you coincide the assault on the citadel with exactly that timing. Are you all right for Friday? It is, of course, important that he is out when you get in. That's the date I've suggested. So maybe then, for the first attempt. Not a storming, no cannon balls, no nothing. Just to see if we can get near. Another recce.'

'You are fucking mad,' Jones said. 'What about me? What about Peg?'

'You neither of you know nothing,' Saul said. 'And oh, I may have the code for the keypad on the door. Saw it from the other side of the street through my bins, took a snap, ha ha. May have changed, of course, probably change it every day. *Tant pis.* You two get in, late afternoon, wait for dark, and then at least get up to his front door.' He stabbed at the map. Three sheets of map, clearly printed. 'Scare the bugger. Like he did with the dog, here. Then get out.'

'It's all with the clothes,' Sarah said. 'Look the part, play the part, you can get in anywhere.'

'You used to this, Sarah?' Jones asked.

'Oh yes,' Sarah said, demurely. 'I've been smuggled into a lot of places in my day. Don't ask. Getting out's the problem.'

'We'll take back his scarf,' Di said.

Jones wanted to spit. You got better things to do here, he wanted to say, and relied on them changing their minds.

There was no communication from Mr Cockerel, and they did not change their minds.

*

Another sunny day, but with a bit of bite to the wind. Di and Sarah were facing a building covered in scaffold in Pall Mall. The view was a variation on what they had seen before. There were three men in yellow overalls, finishing off the painting of ground-floor window frames. She and Sarah were also dressed in yellow with a printed black logo, remarkably similar to theirs, although theirs might not withstand rain. Fishing gear, amended for the occasion. That, and their clipboards, would do them proud, Sarah said, even if we don't have the right code for the door. Six o'clock, Sarah said. They're working late, commute in from Portsmouth, Saul says. They'll be wanting to get off, and careless.

Sarah was definitely on her own territory.

They crossed the road, two bouncy birds. No question about needing the code to get in, there was a man who held the door open. Sarah had red hair spilling out from the confines of her hat. Just checking, she said, looking at her clipboard. Going soon. She was the right age and manner to be a pushy supervisor, super-efficient female, and he waved her in. Know the code to get out? For sure, she said, remind me. Two six eight six, right?

No, miss, that was yesterday. Two six eight seven today, after six. Of course, she said, slapping her head. Silly me. Have a good weekend.

Then they were in the foyer of the old bank, gazing at spaces, the panelled walls, huge windows and acres of floor.

'Latest planning application is for an art installation,' Sarah said, apparently checking off something on her clipboard. 'Am I right or am I right?'

'Perhaps that's what we are. Art installations. Persons in yellow clothes.'

They spoke in hushed tones, slightly hysterical. It was if they had entered a castle, and the walls had ears. Di felt as if she was under a spotlight in a huge, official courtroom, looking at a judge. It seemed to be both dark and light at the same time, light streaming through the windows only accentuating the darkness of the corners. She walked the length of the banking hall, her footsteps soundless on old carpet. She touched the wood panelling, gingerly, finding it warm. She felt utterly conspicuous and vulnerable in all the emptiness. The space was only humanised by a pile of working materials, nesting on a dustsheet in a corner, looking forgotten.

Sarah looked up, pointing out the staircase that led up to the next floor, and thence on, into infinity. They had memorised the plans of the place, but nothing prepared them for this. The silence was astounding. Di tried to comfort herself by imagining the hall full of paintings and people. Sarah did likewise.

'What kind of lunatic would want to live on top of a place like this?' Sarah whispered.

'One with delusions of grandeur. Come on, we've got to find the place to hide.'

It was full of places to hide: their place was selected from the map. The best place to hide was among people, in a crowd, and suddenly Di longed for a crowd. They moved through a fine arch into the second section of the banking hall, where the plans showed two doors on the far side leading down to the basements. They would wait there, providing they could get access, but the fine old doors stood open as if welcoming them in. There were stairs leading down from either door, down, down, down to a place of many cell-like chambers. There was a central block of rooms with a corridor going all the way round the edge. The plan said there were two rear exits leading from the basement, into an alleyway behind. They moved down a long corridor, eerily lit by winking smoke alarms in the ceiling. The doors were all to the left, the rooms behind were effectively safes. Two rooms with wooden doors were more like offices, still equipped with plain deal desks. Receiving rooms, where money may have been counted, goods packaged before being placed in individual safes. A room which looked as if it was purely for the storage of deeds, with vast metal filing cabinets. Any idea of getting out via the basement exits disappeared when they finally found those doors. They were guarded by metal gates, locked and barred. It was so like a prison that Di shivered, hated it with a passion, looked back with longing down the corridor they had traversed. Reminded herself that most of the metal doors stood open, and it was not a prison. It was only a fortress, guarding money no longer there. The plan was accurate: the corridor ran all the way round the box of rooms in the middle; if they kept on going, they would always get back to where they started.

Money and treasure kept down here in safety and comfort, warmed by the pipes running along the walls at floor level. The whole heart of the thing encased in metal, so much metal everywhere. There was a remarkable paucity of exits and entrances in this place. Yes, another entrance to the side of the building on the ground floor, and yes, a fire escape from the top floor, iron stairs clinging to the rear of the building. It seemed as if, once inside, the building was unwilling to relinquish any guest. Essentially, only one viable way in and out, the better way to contain thieves being to imprison them.

'It's not thieves they worry about,' Sarah said, speaking deliberately loudly. 'What's to steal? It's a trap for squatters.'

She looked at Di closely, watching out for signs of panic, feeling nothing but exhilaration herself. She had never been to prison, Di had. Di could not stay still, prowled like the caged animal she was. It was just about manageable, this rising hysteria, as long as she moved. Movement was limited in prison: it wasn't here and this had purpose, while her imprisonment had had none. Eyes adjusting to the peculiar light, she let curiosity take over. Remembered that she knew the way out.

'Don't think much of the decor,' Sarah said.

The walls were painted dull green. The floor was concrete. It was very warm, seemed as if it was permanently heated to repel any suggestion of damp. Inside the yellow waterproofs it was stiflingly hot. Sarah tested her phone. Reception nil. She had expected that. Too much metal.

'So do we carry on?' Sarah said. 'Or do we get the hell out?'

Di shook her head.

'No. We wait, like we said we would. Until we're sure Steven is well off the premises. Then I go upstairs.'

'We go upstairs.'

'No, I do.'

'We'll see.'

They sat in one of the offices and went over the plans. Drank water. Found the loo, waited. A little hungry, but it helped to be hungry, Di said. They were surely under-equipped for thieves, but there was equipment to be found and anyway, they were not thieves. Sarah found two spoons in a drawer in a desk. It seemed funny at the time. Then they prowled again, looking for a place where a man might store paintings. They hate being kept in locked rooms, Di said. They have to breathe. There was a choice of prison cells down here, some locked, some open, as if people had recently left in ragged fashion. Sarah was fascinated by the terrain, following the pipes running along the wall, which grew warmer as the evening closed in. She concentrated on how to open the doors. Di crept back upstairs, looked into the huge room above, to see light fading through the windows. Ah yes, the nights were closing in. Getting dark by eight. She heard the whining of the lift marked on the map, going from the top to the ground, making a sound that echoed deep down into the basement. Only one lift large enough to carry two people, the other lift for documents, jewels, hidden treasures, bringing them down here in a dumb waiter. The quiet became deafening.

236

It grew impossibly warm. Both shed their fishing water-proofs, wandering round in jeans, boots, bright-coloured sleeveless T-shirts and boots, laughing at each other. You must remember, Di said to Sarah, that clothes are impor-tant. Which is why you wear purple underneath the yellow and I wear emerald green. And you must also remember that the most cautious of burglars lose their minds. Be wary of adrenalin, it isn't selective.

'All right,' Sarah said. 'Think instead of the people who worked down here in the bowels of the earth. Were they quiet, or were they noisy? What was the noise like?'

A few minutes to go before they could make a noise, move upstairs. Or Di would go, that was now agreed. She was the one who could open doors. Saul and Steven, meet-ing at eight in the Fountain Restaurant at Fortnum and Mason. Meeting would take one hour minimum. It took that long to eat. Di would try the door to the flat marked on the map, see if it responded to the code or had a lock she could pick – not bad at that, either – come back straight away if she couldn't get in and find the painting, right? You're back-up, Sarah. You get out of here, right? You get out and wait, whatever happens. Those are the rules. No doubt about it: trespassing made you feel intensely alive.

'I reckon the people who worked down here might make a noise whenever no one was watching,' Sarah said. 'And because they were bored and no one could hear them. *La, la la,*' she sang out. '*La, la la la la.* Know this one?

> 'I saw a mouse!
> Where?
> There on the stair!
> Where on the stair?
> Right there!
> A little mouse with clogs on.
> Well I declare!
> Going clip-clippety-clop on the stair.'

Some childhood song Sarah remembered and Di scarcely did, but joined in the overpowering desire to make noise. Sarah banged the two spoons against the pipes, boom boom, clatter clatter, and they both sang and tapped their feet on the pipes, joyful in remembering forgotten words and feeling higher than colourful kites ready to soar.

Got this far, just give him scarf back and run away, giggling. Yeah, yeah, yeah.

That was when Janek came in.

CHAPTER FOURTEEN

This was Janek, coming in early, entering at eight rather than ten, changing the order of his shift because he could. Trying to do one tour of duty before it got entirely dark. He was spooked by this place, whatever SC said. The time that man took him round, making him shout in the downstairs rooms, and given him the key to his own place, had created a purely temporary confidence. Having the key to the man's own flat in his top pocket made him uneasy, open to blackmail. Anything went missing from up there, he knew who stood to be blamed. Leaving off the smoking made him worse rather than better. For the moment, like now, he was more jittery than ever, and even if he knew he brought those ghosts in with him, they were still there. So, as he punched in the code for the door, entered into the vast foyer of this hated place, Janek thought he'd follow the advice and shout and sing when he went downstairs.

The interior alarms were off for as long as the work-men were on site and they had left rubbish in here, like they shouldn't, tut tut. Only the scaffolding outside was alarmed, he knew that, not his problem because another firm entirely dealt with that, promising to arrive with the police within ten minutes if that went off. Keys and more fucking keys, his hands already shaking, telling himself he was not like this in any other building. Start singing then and start making a noise. Only there was a noise already.

It came from behind the panelling, a faint tapping noise which he had never heard before. Louder than the tick-tick-tick of the heating on a winter morning, a sound he had assimilated into memory. It was more rhythmic than that and less consistent; a small, insistent yapping noise, a bit like listening to the beat of someone else's head-phones on the train. He strode through the revolving doors to the first door to the basement, found it wide open. And from down there, echoing up the stairs, sounds of a party, humans or animals wailing, 'Tra lah la boomdiyay!' Ghosts, singing, so that they wouldn't get scared either;

someone else, singing for bravery, echoing among all that metal, maybe metal monsters. That was what he hated down there, all that steel, every surface hard, with metal ghosts who had died counting the money. The noise grew louder, someone making bad music by hitting the pipes that sometimes grew so hot the air down there burned. '*Tralalala, tralalalah*', interspersed with metallic sound. Bad singing in high strange voices, no tune he knew. Hideous laughter as the singing ended, and then he saw them, in their bright clothes. Janek tripped on the last of the worn stairs, fell into their midst and fainted away.

A vision of brightness. One of them was in a bright green vest, a yellow coat wrapped around her middle and she was twirling the sleeves. Bare arms and a face pink from heat. The other one, the taller one, was dressed in bright purple with a halo of red hair. The last thought he'd had before fainting was that they were female and surreal, some kind of supernatural, highly coloured psychedelic art.

'Are you all right?'

A woman's voice, full of concern. A red-haired woman half his size, leaning over him and dabbing his face with a tissue.

'You hurting?'

Yes, his ankle throbbed like fury. Janek nodded. In the dim light of the winking smoke alarms, she had a face like an angel. The face loomed, surrounded by that hair, reminding him of a picture he'd seen, of some kind of angel, only angels did not wear purple, they wore white and this was not heaven, it was hell.

'You the security guard?'

He nodded.

'Nice to meet you,' Sarah said. 'You're early.' He nodded again: he was. She had a voice that spoke of authority.

'Can you stand?'

He tried, lifted up by both of them. They were half his size and made him feel ashamed. Here, one of them said, have some water.

'What's your name?'

'Janek.'

What a handsome fella, the red-haired angel said. Her voice was music to his ears. Yes, he could stand and as he did so, he was suddenly so desperate to pee, put his hand over his groin.

'I need the lav,' he said. 'Got to go. Oh, shit.'

His face mirrored the horror of a child who knew he

was going to mess his precious clothes in public, a private nightmare. That was all he remembered.

You know what? They undid his pants and held him up while he peed through an open door into an empty room. Then they dressed him back, efficiently, tucked in his shirt, sat him back against the warm pipe on the wall, like they were nurses and he that anxious child. One of them closed the door of the room where he had peed so violently while propped between them, the door hiding the evidence, and although that urine stench remained in his nostrils, they never even remarked on it. They were talking among themselves, chafing his hands like his granny, wiping his face, until he began to feel better. Thank God no more singing. They had removed his keys from his belt, dangled them in front of his eyes, not unkindly, just trying to keep him awake. Businesslike, but not exactly ruthless. In an odd kind of way, he did not mind. They were blobs of colour, coming into focus. Two small women, not ghosts.

'Look, handsome,' the red-haired one said, the one who looked like something out of a painting in his native Kraków. 'Can you hear all right? We can get you to hospital and forget about everything else. Not going to leave you down here to rot, not going to leave you at all if you're really sick. But if you aren't that bad, do you happen to have the keys to Steven Cockerel's flat? Or the code? We got a birth-day planned for him, is all. Got to deliver a surprise gift, and get out, that's all. Can you give us half an hour? Then we can all go out and pretend it never happened.'

Sarah was flying a kite: the kite landed.

Couldn't believe it later, that yes, he gave her the key, obedient to her voice. Took it out of his top pocket, and gave it to her. She was nice, even if she snatched it. Never mind how he smelt to himself, he was clean and dry, and this redhead was cradling him. She smelled as good as he didn't.

'Don't leave me down here,' he said.

'Thanks,' the redhead said, drawing him closer. 'You're a star. I'll stay. She goes, and if she's not back soon, you and me's out of here, anyway. As if it never happened. Right?'

'Right.'

He had always been obedient to orders, especially in that kind of voice. Do that and he did it and the sound of *it never happened* was music to his ears. As if this was a dream that could be absolutely forgotten, rewound, wiped clean. He had never been more ashamed; pissed himself in front of two women. She wouldn't leave him. And it hadn't happened.

'Does the door to his flat have a code?'

'Yes, madam, but he doesn't use it. Just the key. He feels safe up there. Only I have the keys.'

He would have given them anything, especially her.

The burglar loses perspective, and hence control, Di told Sarah. When Gayle and Edward came to burgle the Porteous house, they had lost the plot: the danger was always there. You start forgetting the purpose and start lighting fires and wielding axes; you could come to behave like an invading army instead of an individual with a limited scope. You get drunk on success and think you can fly. Di was halfway aware that she was doing the same, exceeding purpose, which was to leave a marker, a sign, a flag of war and to investigate what she could. Di was on an adrenalin high, humming to herself, thinking of old glories when this was fun, like when she was fifteen and divorced from any idea of consequences and conscience, thrilled with fear and the whole sense of achievement that came with the single act of getting in. You have to obey the rules, Di said to Sarah. If the gofer gets in and gets caught, the lookout runs away, runs like hell. If she wasn't half bonkers, she would not have gone, but the key, the key was an irresistible gift.

Up and up, a lift on the map, but she hated lifts, ran upstairs with the plan of the place imprinted on her mind. Two flats carved out of old bank chambers where clerks once lived with their fires and gaslight and duties. Up two flights of august stairs, leading the way to narrower ones. Servants' quarters made grand. A Russian name in Cyrillic on one door, SC on the other. Keypad and a lock, but the Chubb key with the red label on it let her in through a door that was relatively flimsy in comparison to the high doors of the entrance hall and the low, metal doors of the basement. *Doesn't use the burglar alarm.* Well, why would he? Safer than houses up here.

The plan told her that the upper floors were not a mirror image of those below. The door opened, sweetly. She closed it softly behind her. Checked her own mental compass. South that way, west that way. The biggest room would be facing south. She moved into it, via a lobby of closed doors.

Smaller sash windows, for sure, low ceilings, but a long, glorious room, leading to windows and a wall straight ahead, with paintings hanging on it, lit from above. Scaffolding and light through the windows. She walked straight across the expanse of the room, ignoring anything else, towards those paintings. A small grouping, a contrast to the other, empty walls, six of them forming a tableau of seascapes and in the centre was the cavalier. Time froze: Di Porteous was right back to where she was when life as she knew it had begun; when she had entered the house of Thomas to steal from him, and paused. Then and now, she paused to genuflect to a painting, hypnotised. Hello, she said to the cavalier. What are you doing here? Thus she had come into Thomas's life, like this, a thief, mesmerised by a view. And it was as wrong to do this now as it had been to do it then. There was no such thing as a righteous thief.

Hello, she kept on saying, hello.

She sat down, cross-legged, and looked, just like before. And knew, just like before, that this was the wrong place to be. Deceit and infiltration always wrong, even if it was revenge, even if it was justified. She had wanted this man to know how it felt; wanted him to know what it was like to be invaded and never able to feel the same way again. She had his black and white scarf round her neck, the one worn by the dog. The waterproofs were rolled down to the waist, pockets always accessible and her shoulders were bare. Cooler here than in the basement. What had been the purpose? To return the scarf as a message, saying I can do to you what you did to me? Threaten him? Collect what was hers? Yes, all that, not forgetting the paintings stolen from

Granta. Instead, she was sitting, forgetting the time, kissing goodbye to judgement, gazing at the small selection of six paintings on a wall.

Most of this wall was devoted to catching the mood of the sea at every time of day: the sea by night, the sea at dawn, the sea in bright, midday sunlight; all the pictures stylistically different oil paintings, arranged as if the owner could consult them to see what the sea was doing, at any time of day, as he might a clock to see what time it was. Pictures of the sea surrounded the little cavalier as the centrepiece. His indifference to them was palpable since this was an indoor gentleman far more interested in surveying a room rather than a sky. Her eyes went up to painting above him and the one below, then back to the cavalier. What was he gazing at, now that he no longer flirted with Madame de Belleroche? He gazed at the far end of the room and seemed disappointed.

Di shook herself, refocusing, remembering the time. Get out, pretend it never happened. Leave the scarf. Awash with remembrance of knowing right from wrong; remembering the other time she had knelt like this and failed to steal the car keys from Thomas Porteous, paralysed by the memory. *Go, go now, get out*, he had said, and she began to scramble to her feet.

There was a sudden, intense pain to her left shoulder, a sensation of being punched by something sharp that made her jolt forward. A sound, *thwump*, followed by silence. Slowly, she raised her right hand to touch her left shoulder, and felt the repellent sensation of feathers. Then another similar *thwump* to the other shoulder. She doubled forward in pain, hugging herself, pain spreading through muscle. All she could hear was her own breathing. She had bared her back, looking up to the cavalier before she looked to see what he was seeing as she genuflected before him.

'Only a little dart,' the voice said from behind her. 'Penetration less than an inch. You'll live. Next one takes an eye. Not an arrow. Just a nice, sharp dart. Plenty more of them. Stay still.'

She stayed still, head bowed, back exposed, waiting for the next blow. The image of a painting entering stage left, that of St Sebastian, killed slowly with arrows, tied to a cross. The pain lessened. She could feel the vibrations of his feet moving towards rather than hear him, flinched as his hand held her down by her naked neck, braced herself for more pain. He pulled the darts out, one by one, not roughly, easing them out, gently. He touched the scarf round her neck, a light touch. Then, from behind her back, he threw a single dart at the wall of paintings. It landed, neatly and precisely, in the small space between the cavalier and the nearest picture of the waves at night under a moon. His aim was admirable.

'These your only weapons?' she asked quietly, still kneeling.

'No. Kitchen knives and a rope, and things that burn, as well as plenty more scarves to strangle you, only you seem to have brought your own. Bloodied but unbowed, I see. Only a little blood. So far. Take a chair.'

She could not move. The sickening pain eased into shock. She fixed her eyes on the dart in the wall.

'It would be awfully easy to hurt you badly,' he went on. 'I'd be entirely justified. You're the intruder and the law would be on my side. But I suppose you have back-up, or you've seduced dear Janek. And there's certainly nowhere in Pall Mall where I could bury you. So, please do get up and take a seat.'

She swivelled round to face him. Two Perspex chairs, lined up to face the wall of paintings. She had not noticed their transparent existence, nor the table, also Perspex, on which he had placed a bottle of wine, antiseptic wipes and several more darts. He was in one chair, she sat in the other, regarding his profile, listening to his familiar voice. She rubbed her shoulder, brought back her hand with a smear of blood, wiped it on the chair and then pushed her seat back, so that she was further from him. The chairs were already distant from one another. It was not a room for intimacy, not even a room for the view. She looked down to the far end to see what the cavalier saw. A door to something with light coming through. A big painting on the wall. A dartboard.

'You could always have asked me to send the painting back,' he said, raising the bottle and putting it down, as if remembering something. 'Oh, yes, I forgot, you did. And I didn't reply because I didn't know what to do.'

'You sent me a half-dead dog with your scarf wrapped round its neck.'

'I did *what*? What dog?'

'The one you called Grace.'

Even here and now, the memory of the dog called Grace stirred anger, and it was anger she needed.

'What?' he repeated. 'What? That beautiful silly dog?'

'You meant to have her killed.'

He looked at her, disbelieving. Shook his head.

'Came back to my house,' Di said. 'Strangled with your bloody scarf. The one you wore on the beach.'

The scarf was still round her neck.

'I didn't,' he said. 'I didn't. I lost the scarf and the dog.

251

Can I get you a drink?' he asked, like any polite host.
'Something cool?'

'Yes, please.'

He was halfway back down the long room, which led,
according to the plan, in the direction of a kitchen a distance away, seemingly lost in thought, hesitating and about
to say something else, turning back towards her, when the
stone from her pocket hit him square in the face. He did
not fall like Goliath, but put his hands over his face, and
slowly, slowly, buckled at the knee. Blood from his nose
fountained on the wooden floor. He staggered like a blind
drunk, all judgement gone.

Di threw her second stone towards an open window, if
only to hear the sound. It bounced back. Should have run
for the door, gone out the way she came in, *as if it never
happened*, like it did when you played it backwards. He was
making noises, and the halfway-open window called a clar-
ion call. Double-glazed sash, easy to pull up, bend double
and climb over the low ledge, get out. *Get out, get out, now.*
She hauled herself astride the sill, and did not look back.

She looked across and then down, grasped a scaffold
pole within reach, swung both legs over the sill and lowered herself down. There was a wooden platform, guarded
by a guardrail about three feet below the level of the

window. She dropped to it, held on to the rough scaffold and looked down, peering over the waist-height guardrail, the only protection from falling. What she saw made her sick. The next level down was probably twenty feet away, not reachable by jumping, only by slithering down the scaffold pole until she hit it, if she hit it and did not bounce over the edge. And she looked further down into the street, saw the cars and the lights and the buses a huge, huge distance away. Acrophobia struck, the cousin of claustrophobia, which she had thought was her main enemy. Di shrank back against the wall; she could not do this, she simply could not do it. Then, dozens of alarms went off simultaneously, screaming with an ear-splitting, discordant sound, and soon after that, from a further distance, the different, dreaded sound of sirens. She could already feel the prison doors closing around.

She lay down on the platform, making herself as small as possible and put her hands over her ears. Thinking how long have I got? A miniature figure in bright clothes. A few minutes, max, maybe longer. Breathe deeply. You don't want to die.

The only thing to do was go back. She stood up, her head and shoulders level with the window and grasped the bottom of the frame. And there was his bloodied face on

the other side, ready to close the window on her hands.
Only he didn't. They stared at each other and the sound of
the sirens came closer.

Down in the basement, Janek was restless. He had
halfway dozed next to this sweet-smelling woman, and
then he came to with a jolt and struggled upright.

'This isn't right,' Janek said to Sarah. 'Isn't right at all.
She's been gone too long. Do you hear what I hear?'

'Quite right, it isn't right,' Sarah said. 'So, we're out of
here, and it never happened. That's the rules, OK? Come
on, we're out of here. Take everything. Lovely man, you
are, don't worry.'

'You a tart or what?'

'Only sometimes.'

Smiling at him, checking, ready to move. They had
come in with nothing but the contents of their pockets and
the innocuous, empty clipboards.

'Don't forget the keys. Listen, Janek, tomorrow you
take a day off and go to the doctor, you hear? There's more
wrong with you than tranks. Blood pressure for sure, diabetes, check it out. Got the code? OK.'

Out in the street, with a cacophony of sound from hell.
Alarms blazing, the scaffolding pulsing with sound and
light, lit up like a Christmas tree.

'Go,' Sarah said to Janek, touching him. 'Just go. Never happened. You were supposed to be here at ten. Come back then, OK? Like usual? No trace of anything, then.'

He nodded. Limped down the street like everything was normal, light-headed, God was good, didn't look back until he stopped and looked up at the top windows. Steven C was going to know what had happened, even if no one else did. He'd given away his key.

Sarah met Saul on the pavement opposite, huddled in a doorway, both of them breathless, looking up at the noise and the pulsing lights.

'He was supposed to meet me,' Saul said, 'at Fortnum's, for supper. He was late, and sent me a text, saying sorry, he'd be there by eight thirty. Only he wasn't. Then he turned his phone off.'

'He's up there, with Di then,' Sarah said. 'Got to go back.'

'No,' Saul said. 'Those are not the rules. Did you leave any traces?'

'No. We were in the basement, she left her phone, I've got it, she took the key, I've got to go back . . .'

'No,' Saul repeated, pointing to the first of the police cars pulling up, watching the security guard limping back

255

up the road to join in. 'Those are definitely not the rules. We retreat. No one goes to prison on Di's watch.'

Janek had not gone far before he turned back. He wanted to pretend that it had never happened, but shit, there was his DNA in the basement. And there was a wild woman in there with the keys to SC's apartment. Whatever he owed the man, he owed him more than that.

Better he went in with the police than let them go in alone.

They were waiting at the door. Always a quick response for a bank, even one with no money in it.

Had to try and make them see that the trouble was from the outside not the inside, and that nothing inside had ever happened.

He felt amazingly clear-headed, almost like singing.

CHAPTER FIFTEEN

Janek was on song as he led the police in. Four of them in those especially bright yellow flak jackets that hurt his eyes, looking odd under the light of the chandeliers. All lights blazing in here. Identification given and received. They were pleased to see him.

He was explaining that he'd just been in, and done a round of the basements and there was definitely no one down there. But would they come round the rest of the building with him and up to the flats on the top floor, see if anyone was in upstairs? Doubted it, but had to be sure. Told them he figured that whatever had set off the alarms on the scaffolding had to come from outside. Explained that the scaffold alarm had another keyholder who would be along to turn it off from a box on the wall on the outside.

The sound of the scaffold alarm had descended from wailing to bleeping, the way it did after fifteen minutes, so that from the inside as Janek led them up through all the stairways, it was scarcely audible. He disliked the police with quiet intensity, but he knew to be polite. They were far from fit, not even as fit as he was, finding the stairs heavy going, but they clanked with equipment and carried batons at their belts and that was reassuring. They made jokes on the way, blimey, who'd live here, would you, mate? Must be full of ghosts. Going to be a restaurant, I heard. Must be worth a bomb, but is it? Who'd want a place like this if it wasn't a Russian? Lots of them round here. They were unperturbed and used to false alarms, easy for them, they were mob-handed. Janek hoped that if SC did not let them in, they would bash the door down. He knew SC was there. When he'd walked down the street, he could see the light from the window as he went round the corner. Perhaps that was why he had turned back.

Knock, knock, knock. Janek remembered that SC wouldn't even have an entryphone, but he did have a peep-hole in the door. The men in uniform yelled 'Police', in case there was any doubt, and after a delay, SC opened the door. Swept it open and ushered them in, like a host welcoming guests to a party. He was holding a handkerchief to his nose. Affable yes, intensely irritated also. And hurt.

'What you done to your face, man?' Janek asked.

'Played a game of squash earlier on. Old chum of mine gave me a bloody nose, ha ha. Just started to bleed again, when those damned alarms went off.'

He was terribly hearty, not like normal.

'Come in, come in. Has someone stopped that infernal noise? Good-oh, they have.'

He was acting like an upper-class twit, all plummy vowels and rather stupid. That wasn't him, but then Janek was beginning to see that everything about this man was an act. SC led the policemen, who he addressed as 'officers' in the long main room, as if pleased to show off. Janek wondered what the officers might think if they saw a painting with darts in it, but that was well out of sight. Anyway, he led them to the front and that picture wasn't there; others were there instead. One of two front windows was wide open.

'I'm tending to my bloody nose,' Steven was saying pompously, 'and I open the jolly window and all the bloody alarms start. It's not good enough.'

'Any intruders, sir?'

They didn't call Janek 'sir'.

'Good God, no. Been in by myself since the afternoon, recovering from that bloody squash match. Do you play squash, officer? Bloody fine game.'

'No, sir, but I have had my nose broken. It hurts, doesn't it?'

'Yes, it bloody does. Couldn't go out looking like this, could I? Boring evening at home. D'you suppose it was me opening the window caused all this rumpus?'

'More like some drunk, trying to climb,' Janek muttered.

'Wish I had had company tonight,' Steven said, petulantly. 'Some nice bird to look after me.'

The policemen gathered at the open window, admiring the view. Janek met Steven's eyes which were puffed and blackening. *Don't over-egg it*, Janek warned him, silently. His eyes went to the yellow waterproof folded over the chair, to the spots of blood on the floor and the black and white scarf. Steven shook his head, slightly, while Janek inclined his in tacit agreement. So that was the way it was; hear no evil, etc. There was a bit of speaking into phones with the man downstairs seeing to the alarm, the offer of a drink from Steven which was mercifully refused, and then they all went to leave, giving reassurances. Must have been the twit opening the window. Janek was the last to go and Steven tapped him on the shoulder. 'See you tomorrow,' he said, and closed the door.

Back down in the street and while they were not quite shaking hands all round, he hoped to God that SC hadn't killed her. She'd been there, for sure. Maybe a real party. Janek went back in, and down to the basement which scared him not at all. He found bleach in the cleaner's cupboard and threw it over the evaporated puddle on that office floor.

That way, it never really happened, and SC might never know who had given her the key.

See you tomorrow, he said.

Tomorrow, tomorrow, it would all be different tomorrow.

Down in another basement, Jones was angry with them all again. Not only for the ludicrous jaunt up to London which put them at risk, but a failure to appreciate the risks they left behind, which now seemed his sole responsibility. Nine thirty and they'd gone at noon, and not a word, not a text, not nothing. It would take them two hours to get back from that great big alien place he called London, and anyway, they said, they might not get back at all. Do let me know, he'd said sarcastically. All on his own again after another fruitless day looking for Quig. The only way out of misery was to get busy downstairs again. Felt like he was the only person who understood quite what a time bomb the cellar was. This time, he was scrubbing and bleaching and hosing down that back room where the bones of the late and unlamented Mrs Porteous had lain. First he had hoovered out any sign of dust and flaking plaster, then he sprayed with bleach and detergent, then with cold water. Tidied up the rest of the place too, so that it was equally clean. Wouldn't do to have a contrast: one section pristine, the other not. Not that any of it was dirty, merely unused. He paused for thought; it was in fact already as clean as if Peg had done it. They had been avoiding the place, not noticing.

So, if everything looked the same and there was no forensic trace of those bones, Quig's blackmail would be difficult, should he attempt it. The existence of a body and the remaining bones could be denied without peril and Quig could be dismissed as a fantasist. Jones knew that nothing could eradicate remnants such as these beyond the scope of a thorough scientific search, but who would bother? He knew some who would, since Di Porteous would always be a person suspected by the police, but hey, time was money, and Quig was as likely to be charged with wasting police time, if he went that route. He wouldn't. But Quig meant something, because it must have been him who delivered that dog, a reminder of his talents, and none but him could have taken the bones. And that reminded Jones of something else, namely the fact that Quig hadn't even managed to kill the dog. Quig couldn't even kill a dying dog, ill with a twisted gut from eating string and rubber bands and rubbish left on the beach. There were several reasons to be afraid of Quig, and several why not.

Peg came in through the back door so quietly he scarcely heard her at first. Sound insulation between ground floor and basement was not good: voices could be heard dimly, footsteps clearly. They had not spoken much these last few days since the dog, what with all the insanity going on around them, but they were reconciled to a new understanding not yet explored. She was troubled and he ached for her troubles. He wished he did not love her so much. She called to him from the cellar door.

'Got us a takeaway, Jones,' she yelled. 'Want to talk to you.'

Funny how she had lost her fear of the cellar after she had come out of her brief spell in prison the year before. She was not afraid of anything after that. Harder, wiser, sharper, more industrious, with an exaggerated hatred of filth. Perhaps being super-clean was a way of pretending it had never happened, that she had never felt as dirty and as helpless as that, or ever been so stripped of identity that she had to struggle to find another, stronger one. And she certainly had.

Jones went upstairs and washed his hands.

'Got to talk,' Peg said. 'Gotta stop not talking. Eat first, though. We can only have this stuff when they're out.'

Chicken korma, poppadoms, onion bhajis, savoury rice, lukewarm and devoured at speed; a rare treat in this house that insisted on home-made food. They ate in silence, enjoying every bit of it.

'Quig,' she announced, using the last of the naan bread to polish her plate. 'I'm going to talk about Quig. Quig delivered that dog for me.'

He was wise enough to remain silent. Then out it came, the way she'd been rehearsing it, as close to the truth as she could make it.

'I did his hair for him, right? Didn't like the way every-one was down on him, I know what that's like, don't I? Supposing he really did want to put things right? Anyway, I went and found him after that, after that picture went, I thought why doesn't anyone ask him? I can't bear anyone getting in trouble when they didn't do it. Just like you don't and just like Di doesn't, but you both blame him all the time. It couldn't have been Quig took that picture. He just isn't fast enough.'

Jones nodded agreement.

'Was this man they've gone to find, isn't it?' she said, not waiting for an answer. 'Anyway, Quig liked me, and I told him about being frightened of that dog that's been roaming around, frightened of all dogs, me. Don't like the beach by myself, because of dogs. You know that.'

She kept her eyes on the surface of the table, used the tip of her finger to pick up a few crumbs.

'So, anyway, he comes up to me at that bonfire the other night, and more or less said, not to worry about the dog, he'd killed it for me. Or at least I think that's what he said, I was pissed and so was he. Funny way of saying thank you for a hairdo. But it wasn't any kind of message for you guys. It was for me.'

Jones was stunned but he believed her entirely. It was just the sort of perverted thing Quig would do. What he couldn't handle was the idea that it was just a thank you gift for Peg and nothing more.

'Do you know where he is?'

'No, I know which pub I found him in, but not where he lives. He told me he was going away. Got a job, he said.'

She looked up at him and smiled.

'Di's not going to chuck me out if she knows all this,' Peg said. 'I worked that much out. And I am going to tell her, just as soon as she gets back. Just thought I'd tell you first. Quig might be a sad old lech, but he isn't a wizard. And he didn't even kill the dog, did he?'

He wanted to hug her for being so sharp, again wished he could without that being the wrong thing to do.

'Peg, you're the best girl on the planet. And the brightest. And you may have got Quig halfway right, but he isn't harmless. He's stolen the bones.'

It was out of his mouth before he realised he'd said it.

'I mean . . .' he floundered. 'I mean . . .'

'You mean those bones down the cellar I'm not supposed to know about? Only I do. Di wrote it all down, it's on her computer and I read the lot. I can read, you know. And I listen. I know all about those bones and Mrs P who drowned down there when she was trying to kill old Thomas and I know they're gone. And you're wrong about Quig, again. Quig didn't take them.'

She was shaking her head with absolute certainty.

'Of course he did. There's no one else. He'll be holding them to ransom. And if Quig didn't, who did?'

'I did.'

She spread her hands.

'After all Di's done for me, I thought it was the least I could do. I could make you all free. After all, that's what she did for me.'

No one was going to be arrested. Ten minutes after the officers and Janek had gone, silence fell, apart from that ambient London traffic noise. Steven C knocked on the door of the bathroom at the back of his apartment, and told her she could come out now.

It was a nice bathroom, and Di might have enjoyed it in other circumstances, because of the space. Room in here for an army to wash in a generous bath, or for three to shower at the same time. A wet room, rather than a bathroom. She had not protested when he placed her in there, after hauling her back through the window; listened through the door to the opening dialogue with the police at the entrance but not the rest. At any moment, he could have shot her through the flimsy door, like someone once shot his girlfriend, but she wasn't anybody's girlfriend and she had reached the point where she did not care because she was alive, and not peering down into the abyss of the street below and mild euphoria went along with that. What would happen was going to happen.

He had not pushed her, or locked her in. He could have delivered her numbed and shivering self to the police, only he hadn't. He could have crushed her hands on the window but, again, he hadn't. Instead, he had helped her scramble back and led her into a place of safety without locking the door.

Equally, she could have come out of there, all flags flying and claiming assault, showing the strange puncture marks in her shoulders, but she had not done that either. One way and another, they were on mutual risk management. In a strange way, they were now conspirators and it was more than a sixth sense told her that he wasn't going to harm her, or not now. They had bloodied one another and he had not killed the dog.

She had done the logical thing in that soundproof bathroom. Stripped off and showered. Put the same clothes back on. Paused to examine the innocuous contents of his medicine cabinet. Waited. Wondering if this exercise in placing her in the bathroom so near the front door to the flat was giving her a chance to slip out and go. She had not done that, either.

Now they sat, facing the wall of paintings, with the Perspex chairs closer together, and the window still open as if it was still a way to escape. Wine on the table, crisps, nuts. She was ravenously hungry, and was realising that she had never, ever before in her little life, sat in a penthouse flat. It felt like being in a ship, the hum of the machinery that maintained it and surrounded it, keeping it afloat. She could see why such a place was prized, if only for the sensation of being in a vessel quite at home on the high seas of the city below, floating above it. There was no sense of being a captive, or even an inconvenient guest. She ate the crisps and the nuts as if they were a last meal, nevertheless. Steven was developing two black eyes, the inevitable effect of a broken nose. Would be worse tomorrow. The squash game accident, invented when he had been playing the fool, was a good one, she thought. She was full of *why*.

'So why did you do it?' she asked. 'Why did you bring me back in and let me hide?'

The wine was cool and fresh.

'You could have delivered me up,' she continued. 'They'd always have believed you, rather than me.'

'I know,' he said. 'But no one goes to prison on my watch.'

'What did you say?'

'I said, "No one goes to prison on my watch."'

The phrasing shocked her; it was so familiar to her

ears. She had said it so often herself and not always managed to keep her word. She was on her feet, pacing around, brushing damp hair back from her forehead. 'Where'd you get that?' she said. 'Where the hell did you get that phrase?'

'I don't know. Why does it mean so much?'

Maybe it was just the sentiment that did. She wasn't quite listening, came back and sat. Finished her glass, and let him pour her some more, still hollow with hunger, and full of *why*. She pointed towards the cavalier. He had dragged another painting from somewhere else, a large thing, with prominent damage to the face. She ignored it and pointed to the stolen cavalier.

'Why did you steal *that* painting?'

'Because it was there,' he said, quietly. 'Because it felt as if it was supposed to be mine.'

'Like the best of your mother's paintings?' she asked.

'Those, too. They were certainly mine. Can I show you something?'

He hauled into view the big picture, the one of the man in a frock coat and all, with the damage to the hat, and the throat and the black and white cravat round his noble neck.

'I throw darts at him,' Steven said. 'I practise darts on

270

him, I'm very good at darts, like you are at throwing stones.'

He dabbed his blackening eyes with a cloth.

'And I wonder why I do that. My turn for *why*.'

She went across to the portrait of the banker, leaning against the wall, suffering greater damage from the throwing of darts than she did. No muscle behind canvas. She looked at it, touched it, stroked and stood back from it.

'Maybe you didn't like the quality,' she said.

'He reproached me,' Steven said.

'It has scale,' she said. 'It has a bit of style, maybe. But basically, it's a potboiler portrait of some magnate by an indifferent artist. Or maybe not a poor artist, but a bored one. It's been badly relined, but that aside, it had no power in the first place. It's just a bad, over-perfected painting of a powerful man who couldn't see how bad it was because it flattered him and made him bigger than he was. See?'

She swung round and pointed to the little cavalier. 'Compare,' she said. 'That's an oil sketch. But that artist knew what he was doing, or even if he didn't, even if it was a sketch for a bigger thing, it lives, it captures its subject. It captures the room he was in, the world he was in. It's bigger than the sum of its parts, far bigger. Whereas this

271

one is furniture. I wouldn't have thrown darts at it though. Deserves better than that.'

'It's mine,' he said, stubbornly. 'I can do what I like with it.'

'That's where you're wrong. You don't own good paintings. You look after them.'

She sat back, looked at the seascapes.

'Where are you at, Steven C?' she asked. 'These ones are quality. Where are all these paintings you're supposed to have stolen and squirrelled away?'

'You were close to them. Not locked away, that's counterproductive, attracts attention. And I haven't stolen, yet. Sure, I bought below value, but that's business. Only twenty of them down in the basement.'

She groaned.

'They'll die down there. If you don't look at them, they die. And if you haven't stolen anything yet, what about the cavalier? You certainly stole him.'

'It was mine,' he said.

She would come back to that, let it go for now.

'What started you?' she asked. 'Why are you amassing stuff this way? What for? For investment?'

He thought about it. He was thinking about what she said, about not owning a painting. He was, in a strange way, thoroughly enjoying himself. He liked the bizarreness of the situation, as long as he was in control of it, although control was slipping away. He liked her.

'Since you know so much about me,' he said, 'you'll know that I do it purely for investment. My own fortune is ephemeral. I wanted something more solid to fall back on. You can surely apply business principles to collecting art. Buy cheap, look after the investment, etc. After a certain length of time, it pays dividends. Then I watched and I looked for opportunities. I figured that if I avoided the lure of dealers who inflate the value of their own stock, try and make you believe that contemporary stuff is a great invest-ment, when clearly it isn't, if I amassed more classical stuff, timeless stuff down on its luck, I couldn't fail. Provided I paid the lowest price I could.'

She shook her head.

'Collecting for investment only is a mug's game,' she said. 'Because you can never control fashion. Look at the people you bought from. Saving up a painting for a rainy day, and then finding it wasn't worth what they imagined.'

He conceded the point. 'That won't happen to me.' He leaned forward. 'I'm delighted to understand that you know so much about me. I imagine all the information comes from Saul Blythe. He's done considerable research, only he's not very good at covering his tracks. Or terribly subtle. Once he was so insistent on meeting on such a specific date and time, I got suspicious. Then there was something else that connected. His handwriting, the same writing on a little package of newspaper I got through the door, thought it was from my mother, and then his handwriting on his letter of introduction. I just didn't like it. I'm so glad I didn't go. But I wonder if it had occurred to you that research is a two-way street. If Mr Blythe has been researching me, I have been researching you, and I have far more tools at my disposal.'

'Edward and Gayle?'

He nodded. His voice had a nasal flavour, like someone with a bad cold. She noticed, with some satisfaction, the swelling of his nose.

'Among many other sources, including public records, my mother, included. I must say none of these researches prepared me for the reality. I never expected to admire you. Or find you so resourceful.'

'Silly widow who might sell for cash?'

'Among other, more important things.'

Her eyes went back to the paintings. More whys.

'But why?' she kept on insisting. 'Why? Why do you put these on the walls and not anything else?'

'Because I love them, I guess. Enough to want to live with them.'

'Oh glory be,' Di said. 'Tell me about that one,' she pointed. 'There on the left. Sea by night. Tell me why it's a better painting.'

'Because it achieves more.'

'More of what?'

He went up closer. 'Touch, colour, presence? I simply like it.'

'You're there. Doesn't it knock the next one off the wall? Doesn't it beg you to look? Doesn't it make you want to know what else the artist did?'

'Yes, yes, and yes.'

'And what's it worth?'

'I haven't the faintest idea.'

She clapped her hands in genuine delight. 'Glory be,' she said again. 'You could be a real collector, there's hope yet.'

She pointed back to the cavalier.

'And why, in your first attempt at straight theft, did you choose him?'

'Because he's irresistible. He sang to me. I wanted to be like him.'

'A genuine response from the gut. Shouldn't it be like

that with everything you buy? Wouldn't it be so much more fun than all this furtive nailing people into the ground stuff?'

He could feel the conversation slipping further out of control.

'Stealing it might be more fun,' he muttered. 'Only I wasn't stealing from you. As I said, that painting was mine.'

She shook her head as if she was a teacher and he a pupil failing to live up to promise.

'It was mine because my father sold it to Thomas Porteous. It was my father's and I loved it when I was a child. He sold it when I was at school, like he sold everything. I'd always loved it, wanted to be that man in that painting. But my father only dealt in named commodities, and this wasn't, so he flogged it. I'm sure Thomas Porteous paid a fair price for it, but it wasn't what it was worth. I stole it because I recognised it and it was supposed to be mine.'

Silence fell.

'When I chanced my arm and got into your house,' Steven said, 'I knew I'd been there before. For tea, as a child with Mummy and Daddy. I recognised the room. I don't remember Thomas, or it might have been his parents. They all seemed so old. Can't remember how old I was. Young enough to be bored and enraged. Also slightly enchanted.'

Di rolled her shoulders to ease the big, black bruises which had appeared in the bathroom. Only bruises. She looked better than he did, pale and exhausted, stunning her with this new information she was slow to assimilate. She kept quiet, waiting.

'I never went back for years,' Steven said. 'Though it was the place of my childhood and stays in my blood. Never went back because I wasn't the son my father wanted and I discovered I wasn't my mother's child.'

'Any idea who your mother was?' she asked, gently.

'Yes,' he said. 'But no proof.' He leant back, patently shocked at himself. 'Why am I telling you this? I want you to tell me how to become a real collector.'

She could hear Thomas's voice. *Look at anything and everything. Get a basis of knowledge. Succumb to delight.*

The echo of Thomas's voice cheered her.

'First thing to learn,' she said, 'is to realise you're going to make mistakes. Second, is that there is no way that anything is a sure-fire investment.'

'I don't know about that,' he said, smiling with a crooked smile and a grossly distorted nose. 'Look at you. You were.'

She shifted a little, startled at that.

'If you truly love that little cavalier,' she said. 'It's yours and you'd better keep it. Not because it's yours through so-called inheritance or any of that absolute shit, but because you love it. Should you ever throw a dart at him, however, he'll withdraw the blessings he gives and curse you for ever instead.'

'You're *giving* it to me?' he asked, incredulously. 'Why? I thought the whole purpose of the adventure was to get it back. *Why?*'

She considered.

'Because paintings choose their owners. If Thomas had known it was loved by a child, he would have given it back to that child, whatever he paid. That's what real collectors do. Can I phone home?'

'I've done it already. Another bottle of wine? We've some way to go.'

'Yes,' she said, thoughtfully. 'We have.'

A remark lingering in the background of memory.

Granta: *Thomas's father and my husband had the same cleaning lady.*

'Stay as long as you like, Mrs Porteous. As long as you realise I am not a nice man.'

CHAPTER SIXTEEN

Text from Granta Cockerel to Sarah:

> I am not a nice woman. But please, please come
> home and speak to me.

Text for Saul Blythe:

> Mrs Porteous well and safe here. Sorry I missed
> supper. She says go home. Don't worry. No one goes
> to prison on my watch. SC.

'Do you believe him?' Sarah asked, as they stayed, huddled
in a different doorway. 'Last train, soon.'

'Yes. Because of that last sentence, yes I do. Thomas used to say it. Di said it all the time. Do we go or do we stay, sister?'

'Go.'

Text to Jones:

Back by two a.m. Don't wait up.

'OK,' said Jones to Peg, staring at his phone with relief. 'How'd you do it?'

She raised her shoulders, to indicate that it was too difficult to explain. Which it was. She wasn't going to attempt to explain why the existence of the bones in the cellar had been an affront to her own detestation of toxic mess. Nor explain how she was not remotely afraid of handling a skeleton, or how her overpowering desire was to sanitise everything in this house, smash unsavoury enemies into submission, as she had with the bones. They were not repellent to her, even to touch; she could pull them apart, hit them with a hammer without repugnance. They were simply an abomination; they oppressed her; they held the lives of everyone in this house to ransom, herself included, and they angered her. She was not going to say that getting rid of the bones had been a long process, and not all of them had reached the final destination and been crushed to fragments.

'They're only *things*, Jones, come on. That's what bones are, they're *things*. Stuff. Like all this stuff on the walls. Things. Nothing to me. Got a man with a digger to crunch them up and spread them round. They're under the beach. That's what I did.'

Jones thought of the sheer size of the earth-moving machinery used in the flood defences. Yes, that would do it.

'All gone?' he said.

'Yes, all gone,' she said, lying a little, the first time this evening, but true enough.

'What did you do to get that kind of help?'

Peg held up her hand as a warning signal.

'Don't go there,' she said. 'He was a lovely bloke and whatever I did, it was nothing I didn't want to do.'

'Tell me.'

So she did.

'I was watching, loved it all. Some time, when I was watching, I got the idea. All that power and muscle. Saw what they were doing, got sort of hooked on this one older guy who was really great with his machine, but not as good as the other one. Getting frustrated, you know? Dropping stuff, getting impatient and clumsy. Felt for him, you know? He was the one with the attitude problem, and I know about that, don't I? Watched it for hours, even in the rain, I did. Plastered myself against the railings, poking my tits through, was I available, was I? I didn't look at any of the others, didn't fancy them. Anyway, we sort of made an arrangement. Easy: a wave, a pointing of hands, see you later, that way, pointing to that last pub. He got it all right.'

Jones got it, too.

'Anyway, we met. Reckon he thought I was good for a blow job without even having to buy me a drink in that dive. Blow jobs are easy, long as you don't mind swallowing a bit of grit. But he didn't just want that. Said he wanted more than a quick shag, cos I was funny and bright and lovely. He wanted more. Hours of your smile, he said, your head on my heart. Said he'd pay for one whole night. I shook my head at that, no money, I said, we can do all night tomorrow, but only if you do something for me in the morning. Anything, he said, anything. We start when the tide turns, in the dark.'

Jones waited.

'I told him what I wanted, and it didn't seem too much

282

to ask. I said, could you put this old sack of bones down and run over it once or twice? It's my mum's old dog's bones, big dog, she wanted it buried on the beach. Anything, he said. So he carried the bag back to the elephant park, and thought about me, he said, until three in the morning, when the tide was coming up. That's when he started, and I was there, watching. He was first on scene, tossed the bag out in front, crunched it, scooped it up and shovelled everything in front of the water spout. Three tons of shingle a minute coming out of there. All the bits and pieces shovelled round and disappeared. Levelled out later. He was that on fire, he wouldn't have cared what it was he shovelled. And nobody else was going to stop him, whatever they saw. They were into bonus time.'

She looked towards the ceiling, blew out a breath.

'Job well done, eh, Jones? He kept his side of the bargain and I kept mine. Said he'd never had a night like that, and I surely hadn't. Best girl he ever had, he said. And those bones, well they're as small as rat bones, shells, fishbones, bird bones, aren't they? Makes no difference. Stuff.'

Silence.

'Funny thing is, Jones, he looked a bit like you.'

He was silent, saddened, lost in admiration. She would

go far, Peg. And glory be, the bones were gone, and not held by Quig.

'Think I need a brandy,' he said.

'Don't mind if I do,' Peg quipped, relieved of her burden.

Jones sat back down. Trying not to be shocked, and thinking he would slightly divert the subject.

'I reckon you know Di's dad better than I do, by now,' he said. 'You know another man I don't know at all.'

'Don't think so. We aren't mates. Only chats I've ever had with Quig are like I told you and there won't be any more. I was sorry for him, you know? And I was playing God, cos I reckoned he loves Di in his own sick way. "I only want to help".' She copied his voice unconvincingly, but Jones could still hear it.

'And he has nice hair,' she went on. 'I went off him a bit when he bad-mouthed Di's mum.'

'Always had good hair,' Jones murmured, full of reminiscence. 'Good clothes, too, once. A looker. Di's mum wasn't much of a looker, but clever with clothes. Could make something out of nothing. Like you can and Di can't, not in that direction.'

'Quig told me,' Peg said, 'that Di's mum was too good for him and that was the problem. And she only liked cleaning for rich people with nice things, well what's wrong with that? Who wouldn't? And she had a baby before she met him, when she was very young, which doesn't stop her being a saint or give him an excuse to be a bad man. What did she die of anyway?'

'Pneumonia,' Jones said. 'And he wouldn't call an ambulance or let Di do it and she did it anyway and it was too late.'

He stirred the soup of memory and guilt.

'She was picky about who she cleaned for, cos she was ace at it, like you, started at fifteen, worked this house, when it was a school, other big houses. She could pick because she was in demand. People used to give her surplus stuff when she set up home with Quig, and Quig would trash it. *Not for the likes of us.* That's what I remember.'

Peg was watching him drift back in time, nursing his glass.

'Fierce little thing she was, like Di. No one ever knew about the baby and she never did tell. I guess she did what she did, like girls did then. Hid it as long as possible. Some kids just got absorbed.'

'Monica knows,' Peg said.

'Monica knows everything, and sometimes not,' Jones said.

'Monica reckons she got the baby by a man she worked for in one of the villages. And she gave it to him, cos that was the best she could do for it. Or maybe she never had it at all. Different world, eh? This town. Full of blabbers and people who don't.'

'And short memories,' Jones said. 'Even Quig forgot until it suited him to remember. Don't think Di knows either. Oh my word, look at the time. You're done in, you are. I love you to bits, Peg. Don't ever doubt it.'

She raised her head and grinned at him.

'And I'm a sucker for the older man,' she said. 'But not as old as that. Unless he's really fit and driving a bull-dozer.'

Jones stayed at the kitchen table. Counted the years and made calculations on the free paper napkins that came with the takeaway food.

Missed Monica. She was the one he should have married, what a team that would have made. She knew the year everyone was born.

You never really knew anything. You never even really knew a house, especially one of many rooms, any more than you knew a town. So, mercy me, you have the youngest in this house with nerves of steel, smashing bones to bits and no one knows.

Thought of how easy it was to hide a child, or give it away, what, thirty-five years ago?

When were these silly bastards coming home?

Home Saul came, without Di.

Di, Saul said, was busy.

There was a kind of mutual attraction neither of them could have explained. Maybe it was the size of them, each on a level with the other, maybe the freedom of speech existing between a hostage taker and a hostage with nothing more to lose, both of them intensely curious about the other, and in an odd way, anxious for the other's good opinion.

'So what about the dog?' Di said.

She was beginning to understand that the stone had hurt him more than his darts had hurt her, his pride as much as anything else. A black-eyed man of small stature was impossible to fear and easier to talk to than a bigger version, even though, from the other side of the high window, he had seemed enormous and omnipotent. Now he seemed small and articulate and was treating her like a guest, albeit not an honoured guest, at least one deserving more than small talk.

'Don't begin with the dog. Begin with Edward. I got in

touch with my old chum Edward after he failed to sell his paintings. One way and another he told me all about you, even gave me a remarkably good drawing. So, old memories jogged and new opportunities beckoning, I came to see the sea. Speculation, no more, beginning at the far end, planning a four-mile walk, ending with a view of my mother's house. That dog simply adopted me and I gave it a name. Grace, because I needed her. Then it adopted you. I never got as far as my mother's house, she kept pulling me back to yours. Somewhere I lost the scarf. It was a day of colours, a dream, the day I became a burglar. A bit of magic.'

To his own horror, Steven Cockerel found himself close to tears. He stabbed a finger at the whole group of paintings.

'I don't like gifts,' he said. 'I prefer to fight for what I own.'

'More fun to steal or bargain than have it given to you for nothing?'

'Oh yes, gifts don't count. Way too easy. Don't you think that? After all, everything you own was a gift. You didn't earn it, you married it. Not quite the same thing.'

It was a gauntlet thrown down almost pleasantly, and she took it up, wondering at the same time why she should ever seek to justify herself to this particular man, why on earth she should want him to understand, but she did.

'Earning's the wrong word,' she said. 'Or maybe the right one in the wrong place. For another, I don't own anything. Technically, legally, I own the paintings I have and I can dispose of them as I like, but only responsibly. I'm a custodian, a trustee, with a duty to keep these things alive. It takes a passionate attachment and years of training, and yes it's a privilege, but hard-earned. The expense? My life, the foreseeable future, I suppose. And Thomas's death. A very high price. Yes, I think I might have preferred another kind of fighting.'

'You could always sell up, cut and run. Have a life of luxury. Must have thought of it.'

She shook her head.

'Not an option,' she said simply. 'Boring. And irresponsible. And just not an option. I'm a collector, a curator with a collection and a project to spread a bit of joy. Open it out. It's more important than I am.'

He was beginning to comprehend, although not entirely. He was wondering how it was that a young woman who was notably rich should have so little vanity, distracted himself with that thought. Those awful yellow waterproofs, how could she? He also remembered a person who wore silk for a walk on the beach, and had been to prison for burglary of the man she subsequently married. Yes, her wealth was hard-earned, so why was she not disposed to flaunt it?

'And you?' she said, wanting to understand him as much as she wished to be understood. 'How did you *earn* your loot?'

He also wanted to be understood and which of them was holding the other hostage was irrelevant by now. He felt more the prisoner, the man on the couch forced by circumstance to cross-examine himself more than he ever had and suddenly inexpressibly weary. He hurt all over, like someone too long exposed to the cold. The bottle was empty and he had drunk most of it.

'I don't think I've done very much to deserve what I have. I haven't toiled away, though I've mopped a lot of sweat off my brow. I've simply understood what makes a business profitable and when it is likely to fail. You could call it the refinement of an instinct, underpinned by mathematics, knowledge of trends and passionate gambling. All ephemeral, of course, here today, gone tomorrow. No stock, only trade. The expense? Life, I suppose. I want stock. I want something I can touch, something that will accumulate; something I can say is really mine. And you're saying I can't have it, can't own it.'

'No, I'm not saying that. That's my attitude, it doesn't

have to be yours. But you've got to respect the stock. And it's much more likely to accumulate if you collect it with affection. You only have to look at the most successful collectors to know that.'

She paused, hearing Thomas's voice, and her own, repeating his sentiments which had become hers.

'I collect because I love looking at them. It's my chance to see the world through another person's eyes. I can see more, and admire more than I ever could with my own eyes. I can become fascinated with skills I would never otherwise notice, visions and angles and personalities I could never otherwise see, lands I shall never visit. Ways of life I couldn't otherwise comprehend. Beliefs now dead, mythologies and clothes and hidden selves. Life's just too short not to do it. Tell me, Mr Cockerel, what would you have done if you hadn't fallen into the headlong pursuit of money?'

'Geology. I love stones. But there was never going to be any money in that.'

They both laughed.

'Perhaps you should collect stones.'

'Or stamps,' he said. 'Sure-fire things, stamps.'

His head ached and he had drunk too much. There were threads connecting them that he could almost touch, but they were fragile and invisible. He felt as if he was in a play, waiting for midnight to toll, struggling to keep his voice.

'How did you persuade Janek to part with the keys?'

'He wasn't well and we scared him. Believe me, he had no choice. He won't get in trouble, will he?'

'"We"?'

'My friend Sarah. She looked after him.'

He touched his swollen nose and winced.

'Two women,' he said. 'Two women penetrate the bank. Poor Janek wouldn't have had a prayer. You know his dream? Wants to be a security guard in a Bond Street shop, wearing a magnificent suit and looking impenetrable. No basements, no ghosts and a lot of lovely clothes. I want to fix it for him.'

'Why would you?'

'I'm fond of him.'

He said that hurriedly, as if it was a shameful admission. His words were slurring; his eyes full of grit.

'In return for the cavalier,' Di said, 'and because everything has to be a fight or a bargain with you, would you consider giving back Granta's paintings?'

He struggled upright.

'No, they really are mine.'

'We'll talk about something else, then.'

'As long as it's all about paintings,' he said. 'Tell me how to love the wretched things, any bloody thing, purely for its own sake.'

'You already do,' she said.

Then, it was if, suddenly, all the fight had gone out of him. Lack of food, surfeit of wine, injury and emotion bringing a wave of sleep that hit him like an oncoming truck, racing at speed. He fought against it, pointlessly, closed his eyes for a minute, and this time they remained closed. The last thing he registered was her gaze, resting upon him with light, curious anxiety.

His sister.

She watched him closely for a few minutes, taking in his battered features, this time, without satisfaction. She wanted to shake him awake, continue the conversation, but when she touched him lightly on the shoulder, he shuddered, clenched his fists and then relaxed. Did he feel so safe with her that he could sleep? Was this dismissal or a chance to escape? Would he erupt into violence when he awoke, this man who threw darts at paintings and understood so much and so little?

Di picked up the belongings she had brought with her, donned the yellow waterproofs, felt in the pockets for the minimal things she had carried with her. Credit card, a few notes of money, a folded map, a second stone. There was a smear of blood on the back of the chair where she had sat, no more than a smear. She had left a little of her own DNA: there was more of his on the floor. He was the one who had bled the most.

She tiptoed down the long room to the door, closed it behind her quietly and looked down into the vastness of the building. The urge to flee overpowered the strange urge to stay, but the idea of being out, at ground level, made her run, touching nothing as she went, tripping down endless stairs with dangerous speed. *Remember the code for the keypad.*

Outside the great front door, she was hit by the sound. So many variations of sound of gears and engines as traffic breathed at the junctions, voices shouting from somewhere and brilliant lights both moving and static. Di began to walk, a person in turmoil, launched into chaos.

She had a map of central London in her mind, one she had rehearsed and memorised long ago. She had stared at maps on the screen and on paper until they were lasered on to her brain. This part of London had no logic, but she was her own compass; she could memorise and her visual memory was better than good, so that while she did not know the place in any real sense, she was never lost. She had once walked the distance between every major gallery with Thomas, and then he had made her do it by herself. She walked up St James's Street to Piccadilly, on to Piccadilly Circus, up Shaftesbury Avenue, before turning back to the Circus and into the calmer waters of Regent Street, remembering that it would lead her ultimately in the direction of the river. Galleries, museums, parks and the river were her London landmarks. Progress was slow, even though midnight had long since tolled; the streets were thronged in Piccadilly with people both going home and going on, groups gesturing aggressively at already full taxis, all armed for a good time or already sated with it. Ill-clad girls with impossible heels, a queue for a nightclub, litter knee deep, and in doorways, the other variety of humanity settling down for the night. It was not a London she loved, nor the sort of good time she craved. Nobody looked happy in this savage light. There was nothing to compare to the relative serenity of a crowd in a gallery, intent on absorbing what they saw. Not like that at all. Those were the only crowds she liked. A crowd among whom you could sit and stare, peacefully. Her restless feet took her all the way down the Strand to the Aldwych and on to the Courtauld, wishing against hope that there was such a thing as a gallery of pictures that was open all night.

She loved the Courtauld. A private collection, given to the public by a family who had surely collected for love and made their wealth from fabric and thread and clothes. Collected eclectically and selectively, a proper use of money. Given the choice, she would always come here first. Tate Britain would be last, because they owned so much and hid it away. All those wonderful English pictures locked away in basements, publicly owned and never publicly seen at the whim of some egotistical curator. Thought of Steven Cockerel's unloved paintings in the basement of the bank, thought of a project dear to her mind. All those paintings hidden from view, pictures that should be sold, so that other collections could form. Perhaps that's what an honourable thief could do, go in there and steal them, hold them to ransom, rescue them from the dark. Insist that people could see what they already owned, and marvel. If Steven C wanted to be a thief, that was where he should go. She wished she could start over, and do it all again, only this time, go banging on doors, and saying show me what else you've got, not just the cutting-edge thing of the moment. And no, nothing needs to be dumbed down, turned into a child-friendly environment. Children are better than that.

It was late and she was getting colder, and even in her

profound restlessness, in which all thoughts collided like meteorites and burst into colour, and even with the realisation that she was as mad as a snake, she had the insane wish to go back to Steven Cockerel and talk about it. A clock told her it was three in the morning. No trains home, either from Charing Cross or St Pancras for at least another two hours.

Clothes are important, Sarah said. How right she was. Dressed in yellow waterproofs, Di slipped through crowds who made way for her; no designer suit could confer this semi-official status granted by neon yellow. She had walked far, but the uniform allowed her to overtake and walk faster. It would take twenty minutes to get back to the bank on Pall Mall, drawn there by invisible strings. She knew, at the back of her mind, that she could always book into a hotel, but Mrs Porteous had never stayed in a hotel in her life, she simply did not know the code. What would she say? Missed the last train, give us a room, here's a credit card, easy as that, but she didn't want to do it. A doorway was an option for sleep, but she didn't want sleep, only shelter, and all the spaces were taken in this part of town. A cruising police car did not stop, nor would she have wished it. A young woman moving along in yellow was not a victim. She must be doing something useful.

Maybe it was this madness that made her go back to the bank. Or maybe, for the moment, the memory map failed, and there was nowhere else to go. He had rescued her, she trusted him, he had said, *no one goes to prison on my watch*, and he had fallen asleep. She had a fleeting memory of Thomas in his illness, when he gave up the fight and fell asleep in the middle of a conversation, what a mixed blessing it was, to see someone at temporary peace, in a state of trust. All her damaged instincts had been to trust Thomas, all those years ago, just as his had been to trust her. He the suspect paedophile and she, jail-bait. And all her instincts now were to seek shelter with this man, and continue a conversation. Di had been walking for three hours, maybe, well, she was wired for walking. Underneath the stinking hot waterproofs that gave her such powerful anonymity, she could feel the puncture wounds in her shoulder blades turning darker purple and beginning to itch.

Staggering images playing across her mind. Thomas Porteous, Steven Cockerel; two men she had attempted to burgle. Two men who had taken her in.

She turned into the Charing Cross end of Pall Mall, so deserted by now that she felt exposed and ducked into side streets, approaching the corner door of the bank from

Jermyn Street and then ducking back, because there was someone already there. She would have known him from a hundred yards away.

Edward, stabbing his finger at the keypad on the outside and shouting at it. Skinny Gayle by his side, the parents of Patrick, trying to get into Steven Cockerel's penthouse pad at four in the morning. My, my, what a small world it was. In all this whole, huge city they must have been the only friends he could call. And the fact of the matter was they must be good friends indeed, to respond. Old chum Edward, summoned from sleep, his wife beside him.

Those, therefore, were his friends and his allies. Who were also her arch enemies and wished her dead. She remembered what Steven had said. *Edward gave me a drawing of you.*

What a shame, she thought. What a crying shame.

You might have been a friend. Or a brother.

The thought did not occur that Edward and Gayle were drunk, accidental visitors, who had long since been trying to get in. They could not be the mere envious late-night passers-by that they were, seeing a light, taking a chance to get into a place to which they were never invited.

She walked through the streets of London, following her map. Such a small distance in real terms, for someone used to walking by the sea. She measured the miles, no more than six or seven she walked.

Then waited for the first train home. She would never be afraid of this city again. She had seen it naked, been naked in it.

She had to learn to see other worlds too, through her own eyes and not through those of anyone else. She was exhausted, exhilarated and oddly peaceful. Thomas no longer walked alongside her; she walked alone and for the first time she had achieved something entirely independently. She wanted to walk further afield, alone. She could hear him from a distance, saying, Go on, my lovely hunter, go on and explore by yourself. Paris, Barcelona, take a map. Be whatever you are, even if it is an honourable thief. You can do anything.

Make your own judgements and make them slowly. Never accept appearances or reputations, always look twice.

Like you did with me.

CHAPTER SEVENTEEN

Picture. *City scene, circa 1950. Pencil drawing of four men looking at a hole in the road. Anon.*

If in doubt, do nothing hasty, Di wrote to herself in her diary. Looking at maps distracted her.

Five days passed and the summer waned faster.

Patrick spoke cautiously on the phone, talking about more lessons in fishing and telling jokes. He did not mention Mummy and Daddy, and Di did not ask. Next time, can we go out on a boat, please? I want to go out to those sands, want to draw what you can see from there. Seven miles out. I've been reading about it.

Yes, so have I. Jones has it all planned.

Saul had been summoned to London, again. To see clients.

On the fifth day, Sarah and Di went for a walk with a purpose along the coast towards Sarah's village and Granta's house, striding out with a breeze against them.

'We shouldn't have left you,' Sarah had said, repeating it now because walking made it easier to say anything that happened to be on the mind.

'Yes, you should. Those were the rules, and remain the rules should we ever do it again.'

'And are we going to do it again? Please?'

'Never again a private house. That's always wrong. I was thinking of public places that hide paintings that should be seen. Buildings on the scale of that bank, big grey buildings. We don't steal the paintings as such; we take them away, offer to return them on certain conditions. Saul's all for it.'

'I keep thinking about that Janek,' Sarah said. 'Quite fancied him, really. Had an extremely productive time with Janek. Are you still angry with Peg about the bones? Oh, look at the ships out there, the bright white one, looks luminous. Is it a portent or just a boat?'

Conversation went like that on a walk, full of non-sequiturs and interrupted observations. Di paused to throw a stone across the still water. It was hard work, walking on old, rolling shingle, excellent fitness training for the next heist, Sarah said. We'll need to be fitter for when we do it again. It's changed my view of buildings, she said; I look at them now purely as if I was looking for a way to get in without an invitation. I look at exits and entrances and ignore the rest. I've always been like that, Di said, only I'd forgotten. Now I remember all too well. I always think, how would I get in there and how would I get out? She backtracked to the subject before as they walked on.

'No, I'm not angry with Peg, and she knows it. Not angry about that, or about Quig. She was right. I was angry that she took such risks, but I can't deny I'm incredibly grateful. She took away the shadows. Still have to go to the Goodwin Sands, call it a metaphorical burial, without bones. Soon, before the end of summer, before I go away.'

'What, and say a prayer for her?'

'Something like that. She never got what she wanted.'

Sarah snorted. 'Have you?' she asked.

'Oh yes. But I shall have to go away for a while, just to make sure.'

They had rounded the curve of the coast, leaving behind the strung-out houses which faded away in ever descending glory, tailing away into chalets, as if the high point was the once fashionable parade that held the school, then cheap fifties houses, then wilderness for another mile, then the beginning of the cliffs and another landscape. An old/new, single-street village, with an old/new sprawl of houses at the back.

'We're going to see Granta's house, right?'

Sarah nodded.

'She's not home yet. She might never come home, but she's getting there and she's talking. So, I've got something to show you, something to tell.'

Di stopped in her tracks and planted her feet in the shingle.

'You can do the telling right now, please.'

'Steven Cockerel thinks you're his sister,' Sarah said. 'He thinks you have the same mother.'

'Oh,' Di said, although it did not seem to surprise her.

They plodded on, muscles working, Sarah's red hair flying, her full skirt billowing over her scuffed, bright blue boots, looking both dressed and wild, a sort of practical flowing chic Di knew she would never learn. I shall need to know more about clothes, she thought: I need a disguise. Brilliant blue today, maybe green for winter. Yellow overalls might be my signature clothing for when I go away and refresh my eyes.

'Cockerel senior lived here first, for a year in the big house, before Granta joined him. They'd tried to have children, couldn't. Husband presents her with a son, Steven. She falls in love with tiny baby, accepts the deal, and never tells, never admits the boy isn't hers. But Dad does. Dad tells angry, stuck-up teenage son that he isn't so posh, his mother was a slag of a cleaning lady, a girl. Not a nice man, Cockerel senior. Needed to master everything, including art, never got what he wanted, either. If he didn't like it, he threw it away.'

The buildings of the village came into sight. The beach was rougher underfoot, the shingle stones larger. It was afternoon, and the birds sleeping.

'Anyway, Granta never met the mother of the child. Steven's father kept some contact. Told Steven that she lived here, married, had a daughter. That's where all this comes from. The dates sort of fit.'

'Lived and died,' Di said flatly. 'Where are the names in this? Why aren't there any names? Doesn't my mother have a name?'

'Granta never knew her name. Never wanted to know, she said. Thomas remembered her existence, she thinks. Granta thinks you look like Steven. It's Steven who's made all the connections on not very reliable information.'

They came in sight of the small terrace of houses in the village, the only ones facing the sea, the rest of the village hidden.

'But Granta isn't reliable. And Steven is maybe a man so much in search of an identity he'll clutch at straws to build a castle. To find a sibling. Or maybe seek revenge on the mother who gave him away.'

Di thought of her blood on the back of the chair in that high apartment in Pall Mall.

'I wonder if he did anything with my DNA?' she said.

They walked on, the sea louder, as if it had changed voice. There were no fantasies more fantastic than the behaviour of the sea, nothing more unpredictable. Di's whole world was bounded by the sea, which was why she was going to have to leave it for a while and find another compass.

'What would you do,' Sarah said, stopping to watch Di throw yet another stone, 'if any of this was true?'

The stone landed, far out.

'I'd want to tell him what my mother was like.'

'What was she like?'

'She loved beautiful things,' Di said.

It was years since Granta had lived in the big house. The front door of the small terraced cottage next door to Sarah led straight into a living room, cluttered but comfortable, walls full of prints and paintings.

'This is what I want to show you,' Sarah said, in a lecturing tone that made her resemble her brother. 'When I came into this room, four days ago, there were gaps on the walls. There's always been gaps on the walls, or so Granta told me, ever since Steven took the paintings, five years ago, maybe. Before I knew her. She didn't fill the gaps, left the dust marks so that she could see where they were. Yesterday I came back in to check around and hey presto, no gaps.'

Paintings in oil always hypnotised. Di wanted to learn to be captivated by other things, too. Buildings, surfaces, skin.

She was gazing at the whole untidy, unloved display, eyes moving from left to right, down across, then right to left, as if scanning it all into memory, the way she did. Her brain memorised the pictures that appealed, making instant judgements to revise, later, slow to criticise, quick to like, home in on the thing that screamed for closer scrutiny. Paintings could be buried in their own context, Thomas said, the good obscured; looking is a process of elimination.

It seemed to Di that most of Granta's paintings were not her choices, or if they were, they were based on sentiment alone, or a desire to be somewhere else. Souvenirs, a tropical sunset, sailing ships on the high seas, portraits of cats and dogs, and several old depictions of arranged flowers, heavily varnished with elaborate gilded frames, made for a big house. These were the high status paintings among smaller works, nothing which focused her eye as much as those two, small sketchy things of the sea, more subtle and compelling than everything else put together, feeling as if made for her eyes only. Visual memory clicked and whirred like a reverse camera; a smile spread across her face.

'They looked much better on the walls of the bank,' she said.

'Don't get it,' Sarah said.

'I wish I knew what he was thinking,' Di said.

Her face was alight with pleasure and excitement: she was humming with it, irritating Sarah so much she wanted to shake her.

'What is it you see? Why does the horrible man bring

back stolen paintings and not come and see his mother? Little shit.'

'He brought them back,' Di said. 'That's all that counts. And what does that say about him? He could have stolen those' – she pointed at the paintings of flowers – 'valuable, collectable, saleable, but he chose these. Unattributed, therefore far less valuable, but the best. He lies, that man, he lies. He's got the curse. He isn't doing it just for investment. He's got an eye, poor man. The curse of the collector. Oh, good.'

'You can't know his reasons for stealing these two when he did,' Sarah said, getting crosser. 'What matters is his reason for having them brought back. Maybe just because they're a nuisance and not worth enough. Or maybe,' she added cunningly, 'he just wanted to please you. There's got to be an angle. He's not a nice man.'

'He brought them back,' Di said stubbornly. 'That's all that counts. He honoured a bargain.'

'So as long as this ungrateful, over-privileged bastard son likes the same paintings as you do, he's OK, is he?' Sarah said wearily as she locked the door behind her. 'I don't get it. Takes more than that to give a man virtue.'

'No it doesn't, but then I've got tunnel vision,' Di grinned. 'Got to broaden it. Got to leave and come back. You can be in charge. Is that OK with you?'

'There's one way of looking at the whole thing,' Sarah said as they trudged back with the wind spurring them on. 'We won, didn't we? We got Granta's paintings back, OK, with a lot of luck and persuasion, but we got them back. Saul reckons we could get good at this, plenty of commissions like this.'

'Finding the hidden. Stealing it into the light. Getting in, getting out. Liberating art which people don't get to see. You up for it?'

Sarah's delicious laughter floated high into the sky.

'Oh yes,' she said. 'Let's do it again. It's easy. All you need is the right clothes, a pocket full of stones and a map. I'm up for that.'

Jones found Quig, at long last. He was sitting in the bus shelter at the north end, where the beach had changed the most. A square-to-the-wind bus shelter with windows long gone, not quite a shelter at all, but a sitting place with the breeze going briskly through it. There was litter in there, too, old beer cans, Saturday night detritus excluding chips and leftover takeaway quickly devoured by the gulls. It suited its sole, weekday occupant. Quig blended in with the concrete.

So Quig had gone away, had he? Got a job, eh? Yeah,

yeah. If only. Another job, burying someone's dead? Wasn't as if he was some fucking terrorist, he simply dealt with the human and animal litter. He could have been officially employed if he wanted. Look at him, he was looking old and lonely in here and he couldn't even kill a dog. Even the dog had survived him – it was touch and go, but the dog still lived. They all invested him with way too much respect. Quig was fearsome not for what he was, but for what he knew, powerful knowledge, even if it was knowledge without specific use. Quig looked like a redundant man and Jones felt nastily triumphant.

They sat beside one another, Jones as ever itching to punch him, but the energy had gone out of the wish, somehow. Jones really wanted Quig to know that he wasn't needed. Listen, sunshine, he wanted to say, those bones from down the cellar are all gone, have you got that? Nobody needs you to help with disposing of bones or anything else. Have you got that? All gone, gone away, as if it never happened. And would you please leave Peg off your fucking radar, you bastard, and don't go bad-mouthing your dead wife either. Jones wanted to jeer, and then remembered that while Quig might not be lethal, he could still stir enough waves to make storms. And he was a watcher, ever the invisible observer with nothing better to do. Good at it. They sat beside one another in mutual silence, each breathing in the smell of the other, feeling around the sensation, a little like men going into a regular pub and knowing, in time, that the man behind the bar would know what they wanted and bring it.

Still had lovely hair, did Quig. Bit flat today, but hey, nobody's perfect. There was no such thing as a direct question. If Jones was feeling on top of stuff, what with everyone home and happier and Di full of energy, not going wild, and no bones in the cellar, Quig was looking more like a dummy than a man, slouched against the rough wall, with his hands in the pockets of his trousers.

'Business good?' Jones said.

'Not bad.'

Silence.

'Don't need you to take care of bones no more,' Jones said, sticking his hands in his pockets and already adopting the same pose as Quig, body slouched forward, legs sticking out. Two ancient men in motorised disability carriages sped by the shelter, shouting at one another like deaf friends. Friends or allies: something Quig and Jones could never be. Quig spoke slowly.

'I know that,' he said. 'Known that for a while. Knew it a lot sooner than you did. You see a lot, sitting here and there in the shelters, sleeping in them. Much more than you do from the pier. You think you see it all from the pier, but you don't.'

More silence, filled in by the sound of the sea.

'Good spot for watching all them earth movers, this was. Hunker down here weeknights, no one sees you. But I saw.'

Jones felt less easy.

'What did you see, old man? And why did you leave the dog?'

Quig shifted. His instinct was always to deny everything, but it was as if he could no longer be bothered. He jangled coins in his pocket.

'Thought she might like it. I was hired to get rid of the dog, anyway. Dressed it with a scarf thing I found, nice touch, hey? Thought Peg might like that, being the kind of girl she is.'

The desire to punch him resurrected itself.

'Leave her alone, and what d'you mean, that kind of girl? I'll tell you what kind, she's a fucking good girl.'

Quig turned dark eyes on Jones, raised his bushy eyebrows.

'Exactly. The kind who likes handling bones,' he said. 'I watched it. I watched the diggers, changing the beach.

Saw Peg watching, too. Watched for hours, she did, sometimes with that boy, sometimes without. She worked it all out. She got the man she wanted and the man she needed. Sure, she fancied him, that was real, but she looked for the man she could manage. I didn't know what she was doing until I saw him next morning, chucking that sack.'

He paused for effect. 'Mind, I doubt if he'd have spread the bones for her if he'd seen a whole skull in there, whatever she did for his cock. Reckon she's got a use for that skull. Even if a digger could crush a skull, which it could, easy, it wasn't there. She just didn't include it, it wasn't there. She didn't bring along all of them bones. Must have kept the skull.'

The old men with the disability scooters sped past in the other direction, racing each other at fifteen miles an hour as if training for a race. How silly men were without the ruthless guiding hands of women. Their brief presence prevented Jones from screaming and after they had passed, he no longer wanted to.

'It isn't true,' he said finally. 'You're a liar.'

The dark eyes were upon him again, full of amusement.

'That's your problem, thinking that. There you are, bent old copper, thinking I'm a liar? Thinking the worst, thinking I might be after a bit of blackmail, when it isn't me you got to be worried about. Why do you think Peg kept back the skull? Takes one to know one, Jones. She's got you where she wants you, hasn't she? Think about it. Believe me, she kept back the skull for a reason. I'd have done the same. Maybe she sold it. There's a market in skulls, artists and suchlike. No property in bones.'

He coughed and lit a cigarette in a series of actions that involved taking his hands out of his trouser pockets, patting other pockets, lighting the thing with a match from a battered matchbox. Quig, starting another fire and blowing on the flames.

'You don't know much, do you, Jones? She seems to like skulls. She even washed mine. That's not a good girl, Jones. That's my kind of nice girl.'

The urge to strike him, pulverise him into the ground, grew with each breath, exaggerated by the cigarette smell infecting the fresh air, reminding him of bonfires and rot. Quig had done it again. Never attacking from the front. He wouldn't bomb a building, he'd undermine the foundations and that was what he had just done.

'Anything else you want to know?'

Jones tried to laugh, feeling tearful instead.

'Yes, there fucking is. Like what do you fucking want?'

'I'd like my fucking life over again,' Quig said. 'That way I might have got a daughter who loved me.'

Out of the blue, that struck hard; reminded Jones of the waste he had made himself, the wife who had left and found someone better, self-pity for the children he neither had nor deserved. Pity for the cousin who had married Quig and whom Jones had failed to rescue, like he had once failed with Di. And that was why he was going to stick like glue, now. Do what he could for these kids. But Peg, Peg, what was she like? He had a vision of a grinning, toothless skull, kicked into the side of the graveyard, the logical place to bury a skull and Peg would have had the nerve for that, just like Quig. He thought he knew her, and he did not know her at all. Another, awful, thought came to mind, and he pushed that thought aside, trying to distract himself from this momentary empathy with Quig by asking questions, doubting he would get the opportunity again. He pretended jolly, if genuine curiosity, trying to gain the upper hand he had lost. Wondering if he should tell Quig that Di was planning to go away for a while, thought not.

'So, Quig, supposing old Thomas had asked you to get rid of them bones, how would you have done it?'

Quig considered the question, giving it serious, professional attention.

'Bit by bit. Like Peg did, given her chances. Or maybe out there,' he pointed out to sea. 'Only in a few places, mind. Got to be over a well-mapped wreck so the fishermen don't snarl it with the nets. Not too many places left. Not like the old days.'

'You'd never have taken her out to the Sands, then?'

'You joke. Too crowded there already. Too dangerous.'

'Why would anyone ask to be buried out there?'

Quig giggled.

'Only for the chance to drown the fool who took her.'

'You staying around, Quig? Or are you going away? Like you told Peg?'

Peg, Peg, Peg. Playing with a skull. Blackmail. A shifting of power.

'Sometime. Middle East, plenty of work for the willing. Word to the wise, Jones, you know that Edward?'

Jones nodded, feeling sicker and sicker. A strong breeze, more than suggestive of autumn, struck the back of his neck through the gaps in the shelter and wafted cigarette smoke up his nose. He longed for the smell of fish and the feeling of power that came from being on the pier where you could see everything and nothing.

'He keeps in touch. Wants information, doesn't want to pay. Asks me to keep an eye, started up again asking, recently. Tell Di that it ain't all over yet. And tell her that those kids of Thomas ain't ever, ever going to know about them bones. Not from me. As long as she don't let me starve.'

'She never would let you starve, Quig. Or go to prison on her watch, either. Whose baby did her mother have, Quig? Before she met you?'

'Did she?' Quig said, his dark eyes innocent. 'Well, bugger me. Blessed if I ever knew that.'

Jones left him there and walked the mile home, watching the pier hove into sight, his place of refuge, his comfort zone that was not so comforting now. Quig saw more at ground level than he ever did from the pier. There was no doubt about it, Quig had won this round. He was still a player, Quig.

Steven Cockerel studied images on his screen. Here was a depiction of a skull. Not the Damien Hirst skull, the famous one, ostensibly purchased by a mysterious consortium of buyers for millions of pounds, made of platinum and studded with real diamonds, but another one, by a near contemporary, made of soap and wax, covered with cheap crystals and all the better for not being real. Attractive, artificial piece for a lover of glitter, but you couldn't wear it.

He touched his own, delicate skull and wondered if it still contained a brain, and what interest was there in the shape of any skull without that grey matter inside, without eyes and lips and hair? Skulls were receptacles, was all, certainly made of permanent stuff and might look good on a certain kind of nihilistic home. There were mausoleums full of skulls. Bones and horn once used for buttons, more useful that way, better still left in peace. And why would you ever want a decorated skull when you could buy a portrait of a living face?

His own skull was bruised. The stone thrown by Mrs Porteous had fractured the bridge of his nose and the skin round his eyes was a kaleidoscope of colours. The eyes themselves peered out of his face as if they belonged to someone else, looking back at him with fierce intensity, proof that he was thoroughly alive.

That was what you got from a portrait; you got a person, a whole life. He had learned from looking at por-traits that as often as not, one of the eyes in the painting was dead centre, the focal point in the whole composition. In others, the eyes gazed out, to follow the observer round the room wherever they stood or moved, while some of the best portraits did not focus on the eyes at all, and seemed to avoid the face. It could be a portrait of the back of the head, or the head half turned, apparently featureless, not revealing the whole face, but making you long to see it. You could recognise that person and follow them down the street by knowing the back of their head. Want to say, Hey, turn round, let me see you, I know you already. You wouldn't want to do that to a skull.

No profile.

Ten o'clock at night, and Janek came in. He looked into the long room, where that little man sat facing his screen, so small he could have throttled him or struck him over the head. He was presenting his stooped back near the windows, with the light on his face. Lonely man, with his computer usually out the back, now moved to the front, facing that wall of paintings with the two gaps in it, so that it looked out of order.

'So, you did it all right.'

'Did what you said. Nice day out. Taxi all the way, easy to get in. Day out by the sea, no problems. I come from the sea, liked it. Why don't you go and see your mother? Nice house.'

'She isn't my mother.'

'Yeah, yeah. She just raised you. You talk in your sleep.'

Steven did not turn round, in case that should indicate affection.

'And what did the doctor say?'

'Got diabetes, haven't I? Under control, explains a lot of stuff.'

The fingers at the keyboard paused.

'Would you rather work by the sea, or in Bond Street?'

Janek sat on one of the transparent chairs.

'You trying to buy me?'

'Can't buy anything today.'

Janek looked at the skull on the screen. Weird stuff, art.

'Got any mates calling round later? Like those drunks hanging off the keypad when I came back the other night? Man that was a wild night.'

'Not friends,' Steven said. 'Opportunists. Casual callers. I owe you.'

'No you don't. Anyway, you want the news? News is there's a whole bunch of people coming in now the work's done and the scaffold's down. Three different planning applications, people coming to look, sort of open days. Anytime soon.'

'What a bore,' Steven said. 'Though I couldn't have sole occupation for ever.'

When Janek had gone, Steven moved away from the screen and consulted the damaged painting of the old banker. You would never have wanted to follow him down the street. The balance of power was always changing; servants became masters and masters became servants, always the same. He had found a new master. He consulted his crumpled little sketch of Diana Porteous. More life in that drawing than acres of listless paint. He would follow that one down the street. He would want her to turn back.

Took a while for a DNA test on blood and hair to prove results. And suddenly, it didn't matter, either way. She might be his half-sister, she might not; he would still want her to turn back.

He went back to portraits. Found a website where he could examine thousands of oil paintings in public collections, 80 per cent unseen and hidden away. Fancy that. There was a real project for a certain kind of thief. He touched his displaced nose, and then his chest. Heart ache, brain ache, everything.

Thought about stones and sea and fingered the stone she had left behind, more lethal than any of his darts.

Then he emailed his mother.

Just to check in. After all this time. Thanks, Mother.

Whichever way it is, I've found her.

What do I have to do to be a nice man?

I want her to teach me how to throw stones.

CHAPTER EIGHTEEN

Daniel the boatman said he would know twenty-four hours before if the wind was going to change. Bigger and faster vessels could take greater risks than his. The wood-built fishing boat was a safe old plodder, well able to deliver, and incapable of outrunning a gale. He took no one out there if he could not bring them back. Jones trusted him all right, but no one in their right minds trusted weather.

Looking out from the top window through Jones's binoculars on the day before, watching the line of foam on the hidden sands and imagining the size of the waves, Patrick had a secret hope that tomorrow afternoon would not happen, or that his mother would retract her permission.

She had been asked and she had agreed; always anxious that he would do something a little more manly than drawing stuff, while his father wanted him to be a team player. It was surely going to be a rite of passage of some sorts, going out there: he would be a different person when they came back; taller, maybe, braver and certainly not the same.

Jones showed him a picture of the boat and Peg showed him stuff on her iPhone. The boat seemed criminally small in comparison to the tankers seen on her little screen, as tiny as those other fishing boats he had seen from the pier, bobbing about, surrounded by gulls and a fraction of the size of a cargo ship further out. Tiny, in proportion to the distance it would travel, and there was something scary about travelling out of sight. So, he wanted to go, he was immensely excited about going further than his eye could see, and he wanted to see whatever he could see from out there, looking back. At the same time, he wanted it over and done with, wished he was on the other side of it.

No message of cancellation came. Patrick fingered the little ceramic frog which he always kept in his pocket, his lucky charm, given to him by Grandpa. It made him brave.

Jones was another one who wished it would not happen, almost prayed for it, and yet the appointed day dawned bright, clear and calm, with an autumn nip in the air. Embarkation time noon, return about five in the afternoon. One hour at least for getting there, half an hour for getting off Daniel's boat into the tender dragged behind like a disobedient dog snapping at a rope; an hour and a bit to explore, another hour or more to return before the tide came creeping back underneath and filled in the footprints. Patrick had asked if they should take food for the seals which might be there, basking in sunshine, and Di said no, only food for ourselves, unless he wanted raw fish.

How much food? Patrick said. A lot, she said.

How many of us going? Patrick said. We'll see, she said. The only people to go are the ones who want to go.

Daniel's boat took six, possibly eight, all of them sitting around the edges up front. In the end, the Porteous party consisted of Di, Patrick and Sarah, accompanied by another party of three strangers. Fine by Patrick, who worshipped the crew on sight, Daniel with a beard and a belly and another man without teeth but plenty of hair who promised him he could drive the boat on the way back. Disappointment that Jones was not coming faded quickly;

here was plenty of male protection. No one ever expected Saul to join in. Jones said he would keep the home fires burning and watch from the pier. Peg said she wouldn't be seen on that boat, because it stank and never travelled anywhere without a rancid dog. So there they were, sitting up front with three unknowns making up the numbers, wearing cameras round necks, dressed for the cold in hoods and scarves.

This old boat was winched down a log-built runway into the sea off the steep shingle slope where the last of the fishing boats lived. The furniture for guests was rudimentary; a couple of seats on the sides, three rickety canvas chairs. The camera-clad tourists already clutched at their hats, and once they were launched, Patrick lost all fear. From here, you could see shore, the houses minimalised but beckoning safely as if a touch away. From the back of the boat, watching forward rather than back, he could see with his naked eyes that there was a man waving from where they had embarked. Everyone else was at the front, staring forward, while he waved back, exhilarated by the retreat as much as the advance.

Jones trained his binoculars on Daniel's boat from the pier before it was beyond his scope. He could see every detail for the first half mile and the bright sun blessed him. He could see what he thought was Quig's head emerging from the hold for the fish, like he was one of the crew. The head ducked down again. Not Quig, only someone like Quig. Jones was paranoid as well as superstitious. Oh shit. He had a horrible conviction that out of this voyage to the Sands there was someone who wasn't going to come back. Fuckit. Daniel registered all passengers with the lifeboat before he set out, numbers, not names. All right then.

The horizon was full of passing vessels. *Minerva* to Rotterdam. *Gladys* coming into Ramsgate. A vessel bringing stone from Rotterdam to Dover en route to somewhere else. Of course they would all come back. Daniel had never lost a soul.

Once the boat was further out he would not be able to see them. Raising the binoculars to his eyes one last time, Jones swore he could see a man's black and white scarf. A small man at the prow of the boat, talking to Di. Warm out there. Hats off, personalities revealed.

A man with a black and white scarf, before they all faded into the distance on a bright blue day.

Peg was at work.

In Monica's hairdresser's, it was half-day closing and she was using the time to practise techniques like any good student, setting the hair of a wig on a stand, putting in the rollers, giving it style. Had to do this again and again to get it right. Other people knew about art: she wanted to know about hair. Peg abhorred any object that was not useful. She was practical to her own bones and this was a perfect use for an object.

There it was, the skull, painted gold, wearing sunglasses and adorned with a russet wig, the perfect shape to teach her the irregularities of the head in a way the wooden model just didn't. When you washed hair and massaged a head, it wasn't wood or plastic you felt, it was bone.

Painted it gold with spray paint, put it on a stand made out of a stick of driftwood, anchored on a base of powdered plaster, mixed with water and left to dry, there you go. As well as all that, the head sat at an angle, never straight, like all heads did in front of a mirror.

Peg thought it was extremely stylish, although she kept it away from the window.

Anyway, live models were hard to find.

Got a text from a man in Rotterdam.

Coming back soon with bigger stones.

ACKNOWLEDGEMENTS

Thanks to Prosper Devas, map maker, for all the ideas and plans.